D0208844

CORPSE
-OF-
FREEDOM

A Books on Fire Publication

Copyright ©2008 Lloyd Garner and Dax Garner

www.CorpseofFreedom.com
www.BooksonFire.com

Library of Congress Control Number: 2007939566

ISBN13: 978-0-9779186-9-0

Lloyd Garner Photo ©2007 Marisa Schibilla
Dax Garner Photo ©2007 Dennis Kwan

Manufactured in the United States of America

First Edition: February 2008

10 9 8 7 6 5 4 3 2 1

for **Marnie, Leeman, and Evan**

CORPSE
-OF-
FREEDOM

--------------AN AMERICAN NOVEL--------------

DAX
GARNER

LLOYD
GARNER

BOOKS ON FIRE • PHOENIX, ARIZONA

"Why stand we here idle? What is it that gentlemen wish? What would they have? Is life so dear, or peace so sweet, as to be purchased at the price of chains and slavery? Forbid it, Almighty God! I know not what course others may take; but as for me, give me liberty, or give me death!"

Patrick Henry - March 23, 1775

PROLOGUE

RYAN KNEW HE WAS IN THE TRUNK OF A CAR because the stuffy odors of gasoline and grease were unmistakable, and he could sense the slight bounce of the coil springs. As the motion of the vehicle kept him sedate, he welcomed the throbbing pain at his temples. He embraced the miserable ache in an attempt to experience all he could, before what would surely be his demise.

While his friend lying next to him was still motionless and probably dead already, Ryan pretended the warm blood on his lips to be a blueberry kiss, then let his imagination drift further into the darkness. Images bubbled up from the back of Ryan's skull and through his eyes. His memories coalesced in front of him so he could relive his regrets, fears, and passions one last time in color. He watched the warrior, the angel, and the corpse all dance together, mocking his desperation, until he could no longer keep the images from his mind's eye together, and they all dissolved and went back to wherever they were created.

How exactly did it get this far? Not even a week ago, the world was an indefinite bore-circus of teenage tedium. The endless pursuit of pleasure in the land of comfort. Not even a week ago, he was an entirely different person. Well maybe not much different at all, but he felt he was on the verge–the razor's edge–of learning a cosmic truth about life.

Now tomorrow would never come, and even if he had fully understood that gem of knowledge, he would be unable to utilize it. Too bad he wasn't smart enough to have learned faster. He wondered if at the split second before the end, whether it would all be clear. All the secrets of the universe crystalline in his consciousness for one brief moment and then it would be over. The irony was too typical to be funny. He doubted he would want to know all the details about everything anyway.

And yet, if he could go back to the beginning and do it all differently, he wouldn't. He needed to make the first step before he could take his last, and he would rather live one second boldly, than live a thousand lifetimes in a heartless muddle.

Ryan thought about how things were so empty and childish in the beginning, and then he felt the car come to a stop.

1

BLANKETED IN THE COMFORTABLE RAINBOW OF brown, Everdale, USA has developed to the point where it is now best described as a suburbanopolis: one massive blob of beige neighborhoods, and progressive commercial centers coated in the same dirty uncolor.

Upon the seasonal wind that sweeps through the city, rides a change; or, a promise of possible change, called a choice. To the youth who dwell within the city's milieu of dullness, this choice is given. For the mature, their choice was already made–in their time.

"Grab your sledgehammer," crackles Arno's voice from the other end of the phone. "We'll need it."

"Yeah?" Ryan asks into the cordless receiver tucked against his shoulder. He shakes off a sudden chill that runs up his spine with a spare thought that the garage should be better insulated; due to the fact it was almost completely filled with the type of useless clutter even Goodwill would reject.

With a grunt, he continues shuffling through a mass of old clothes that spill out of a large cardboard box. "What do we need that for?"

"Kerry said to get one, so," Arno drags a long distracted 'Uh' over the line, then says, "I'm just relaying the message."

"What about shovels?" Ryan's phone produces a piercing static squeal. "You guys have some–" Another squeal and he almost tosses the phone. "Arno! What the hell is that noise?"

"Noise? Must be bad reception. What time can you pick me up?"

"Well, I need to go by Jalisco's." Ryan pulls an old turtleneck from a box labeled 'Costumes + Stuff'. It looks black, but the single hanging light bulb makes it difficult for Ryan to determine if he can use it or not. "You know, for some other supplies first."

"Jalisco's, huh?"

"Yeah, you want something?" After pinching a couple beads off of the sweater's glued-on design, Ryan figures it will have to do.

"Feeling charitable?"

"What's Kerry bringing?"

"Denise," Arno sighs. "Maybe a treasure from his parents' stash. But don't count on it."

"So, are we really going to do this?"

After a brief silence, "Why not?"

"You know how people like to talk a big game and then back out when it comes time. I'm just tired of being disappointed."

"Do you want to *rock*, or what?"

"Of course," Ryan says without hesitation. "I think it's gonna be awesome. I just didn't know if anyone was backing out or anything."

"Yeah, well, hurry up."

"Alright. I'm leaving in a minute." Ryan hangs up on Arno's farewell. He pulls the turtleneck sweater over his head and checks himself in a beer mirror entitled 'American Bald Eagle' that hangs above a shabby workbench. At first he thinks he looks like the classic cat burglar, which is pretty good in his opinion, but then he cringes when he realizes he looks more like a mime, or a gay theater director. He pulls some more of the bedazzled accents off of what he now recognizes must be a women's sweater. *It will have to do.*

He reaches for a pair of weight lifting gloves from the workbench he had set aside earlier and slips them on, then he pulls a black ski mask from a nail embedded in the wall and puts that on too.

Ryan's head swirls in a dizzy fever of excitement and his gut twists with the dread of imminent doom. He's heard people say they have a fire within them, and he thinks this euphoria washing through his veins may be something like that. A rage of fear and anticipation in his chest so ferocious and thrilling it almost suffocates him. Under the dim light, he reassesses his disguised appearance in the bar mirror with dark satisfaction. *No one will know it's me.* Ryan smiles at himself. *I could be anyone.*

2

LIFE SUCKS THEN YOU DIE IS THE PHILOSOPHIC EPITAPH that someone has scribed with black permanent marker on the upright granite gravestone for one Paul E. Radcliffe; loving son, brother, and putrid carcass. Ryan, masked and gloved, gestures to Mr. Radcliffe's headstone with his round point shovel.

"What about this one?" He looks to Kerry for confirmation. Kerry is garbed in what he normally wears, a collared shirt and jeans. He didn't dress for the occasion like Ryan.

Kerry uses his flashlight to read the grave, snorts at the vandal's inscription, but shakes his head. "I don't like him."

"What's the difference?"

Kerry is already continuing his search. "I'm just not feeling it."

Ryan turns to see Arno standing a few yards away carrying a pickaxe in one hand and a long handle sledge in the other. Arno sways back and forth in front of a large statue of a man with his fist in the air.

"Hello, Jesus," Arno belches to the cemetery 'feature' he is admiring. "Hey guys," he calls. "I found Jesus!"

Denise grabs Arno by the collar and threatens him with her crowbar. "Shut the hell up, you drunk *idiot!*" she hisses as she shoves him away.

Arno didn't bother to dress for the occasion either. Neither did Denise. She's wearing a dress. To Ryan's mild disappointment, it seems like he is the only one in the true spirit of things.

"Here!" Kerry proclaims, waving his flashlight to direct the other three to a shadowy area of the Everdale City Cemetery. "It's perfect," he judges.

"How deep do you think it is?" Ryan asks from behind the ski mask.

"Six feet," Kerry replies. "That's what they say anyway." His tone dismisses both the question and answer as irrelevant. "All I know is what I hear in music and movies and shit, okay?"

Arno blatantly disregards Denise's warning for silence by wielding his tools in some sort of drunken kung fu. "This is awesome!" he hoots as he smashes off the serene head of a plaster cherub with a wild swing of the sledge.

Ryan drops his shovel on the ground, pulls a tall can of beer from his jacket and cracks it open.

Kerry picks up Ryan's discarded shovel, his eyes glittering with excitement as he clenches it with both hands. "We'll have to work real fast if we're going to get out of here before sun up!"

"Hold on." Denise pushes her way past Ryan. "Let me see."

"Shut up, skank!" Arno scolds her, with a finger to his lips.

"Hey!" Kerry jabs Arno in the ribs with the shovel. "Don't talk to her like that, queer," he warns.

From behind Kerry's protective shoulder, Denise throws Arno a nasty look, and Arno returns it with a glare.

"Why here?" Ryan asks, ignoring the bickering.

Kerry points to the gravestone as if fate has stepped in. "Well come here, check it out," he says proudly.

Ryan takes off his mask and kneels at the grave marker Kerry had picked out. It reads:

HE LIVED WITH THE HEART OF AN EAGLE

JEFFREY C. NEIL

JUNE 21, 1980 – FEBRUARY 6, 1999

"Died nineteen ninety-nine," Ryan breathes. He slurps his beer and turns back to see Kerry and Arno already digging. "Do you think he's pretty rotten?"

"I'm sure this thing's *ripe*," Kerry replies as he rapidly tears up the turf. "But you're not seeing it."

"February six is tomorrow," Denise chimes in.

"Well technically it already is," Kerry corrects. "I *said* it was perfect. We'll give him a birthday party."

"Dumbshit," Ryan lashes, "he *died* February six."

"Whatever. *Re*birthday, then." Kerry cranes his neck, looking in all directions. "It's good too, 'cause no one will see us here."

"This guy was like our age." Denise hugs herself in discomfort.

Kerry stops to wipe his forehead, already dripping with sweat. "Come on, Denise. This is *fun*." He makes a weak attempt at hugging his girlfriend, but she breaks away.

"I know, Kerry. I don't have a problem."

"Good, then you can get to work," Kerry says, planting the shovel in the soil with a stomp. "We could be digging for a while."

"How long?" Denise whines.

"Well baby, the faster you help, the sooner we can leave."

Arno hoots in delight, working franticly with the pickaxe.

"Close your mouth, pud," Denise tells Arno, but he is too focused to pay her any mind.

Kerry returns to the thrill of the evening. "I bet it's full of maggots and fun shit!"

"It's probably just going to fall apart," Denise says while holding the flashlight for Kerry.

Ryan looks up to the big moon that gives a perfect glow for the night's planned excursion, and breathes deeply, swelling his lungs with the brisk air. *This is the best.* He takes a large gulp from his tall boy and surveys the cemetery through the nice buzz he has achieved. "How long does it take for a body to turn to dust?"

Kerry looks at Ryan with irritation. "I don't know. I'm not a scientist. Can you riddle me this? Why are you standing there thumbing your ass?"

"You have my shovel."

Kerry takes a ragged breath and offers the shovel to Ryan. "Here. We'll take turns," he pants.

Ryan downs the rest of his tall can and tosses it in some bushes, then takes the shovel from Kerry. "Just thought you'd done the research."

Kerry shrugs, struggling to dry his face with his shirt. "It *shouldn't* be dust."

"This better *not* be dust," Arno grunts. "I'll be pretty pissed if I wasted my whole night digging up nothing."

"Just keep digging, homo," orders Kerry.

As he plows the shovel into the soft earth, Ryan's eyes drift back to studying the grave marker. *Jeffrey.*

3

SAILING ALONG THE WIDE AVENUES OF EVERDALE, 'The Defiler'–Ryan's appropriately named 1980 Chrysler Newport– roars through the sleeping city streets as a thunderous booming spectacle of misappropriated horsepower. Supported by a pair of headers, glasspack mufflers, and an Edelbrock carburetor kit, the dark heather brown sedan delivers shockwaves of noise from its suped up 5.2L V8 while spouting billowing clouds of carbon dioxide out the dual exhaust.

Denise sits in the passenger side of Ryan's pet car with sandy grit in her hair, drinking from a bottle of Strawberry Cream MD 20/20. She offers it to a filthy-faced Kerry, but a grime-covered Arno intercepts the bottle.

"Give us a drink!" Arno hollers like a toothless tramp at a freeway offramp. "Here Jeffrey, you look a little dry." Arno tips the bottle to the fifth passenger that sits between himself and Kerry: a decently preserved, sunken-faced corpse.

Arno presses the lip of the bottle to clink against the corpse's fetid teeth and splashes some of the contents against the inanimate mush-face.

Kerry snatches the bum wine from Arno before it can be spilt further. "Don't ruin the man's suit, Arno. It's all he's got." Kerry flicks a black speck off the mouth of the bottle before taking a drink.

Ryan tries to wipe off some crud from his brow, but is unsuccessful because his gloves are covered in dirt. To Ryan, the adventure is more intoxicating than any alcohol, and as he races along, he drinks the merriment of the moment like it was heaven sent ambrosia promising eternal life.

His bliss cracks as his mouth fills with a fog of male stripper stench. Arno has taken out his can of body spray and is liberally hosing the corpse from head to toe. "Are you done?" he asks, opening the window to catch a fresh breath.

Arno applies a couple more quick sprays. "I'm just helping him out."

"That really smells rank," Kerry tells him.

Denise turns around and tries to snatch her sweet wine from Kerry. "Don't drink it all!"

After taking a gigantic swig, Kerry hands back Denise's beverage with a, "Here baby."

"A-hole." She takes a ladylike sip of the half-gone bottle while searching the radio for some music. "Oh yes! Yes! Yes!" she squeals when coming across an average bubblegum pop operatic. "Leila!"

"Leila Caverns sucks shit," Arno declares.

Denise responds by turning the radio up until the thumping music distorts through the rattling sound system.

"Turn that trash." Ryan reaches for the radio, but Denise slaps his hand away and gives him an admonishing look. "It's my car, Denise."

"There's nothing else on," she soothes off-handedly. She is busy grooving to the tunes, already mouthing the words without a care if anyone else is enjoying themselves or not. When the chorus hits, Denise screeches along with the track, "It's like doctor, uh huh! I'll show you mi-ee-eye-eene, yeah."

All Ryan can think is, *Wow. That's the worst thing I've ever heard.*

Arno joins in the sing-along, loudly overdoing it with grandiose gestures and mock emotion. "Deeper oh ohh! Yeah, deeper in mine," he wails.

Ryan cringes from the over utilization of the vocal range. He tries to distance himself from the situation mentally by studying the corpse of a young man in his rearview. The first thing that strikes him is the size of its teeth. They look big, but it's probably because the lips have shriveled away. The eyes are almost closed, but slope inward, and its hair looks fake, like a wig. It must have been almost glued in place with hair spray. Overall, it seems that most of the moisture has been sucked out and then someone fiddled with its face a little.

Kerry howls like a wounded dog in his interpretation of the Leila song.

"Everyone shut the *hell* up!" Ryan screams, but his friends continue the sing-along up to the song's close.

Arno leans into the front seats. "Hey, let's get some burritos Ryan. You hungry? I'm famished."

"Jeff's wasting away back here," adds Kerry with a drunken slur. "He needs a *pollo especial*…stat."

"Quickies?" Ryan asks the car.

"What else is there?" Arno points out.

Ryan ramps over the sidewalk as he pulls into the drive-thru of one of the only twenty-four hour restaurants in the vicinity, Quickie Food UnLTD.

"Curb check!" Denise laughs.

Quickie Food is a generic franchise that has a joyous turkey named Gibbles as a mascot. Ryan doesn't know why the turkey is so happy to be eaten, or how the mascot is supposed to make him hungry, and he guesses he may never know the logic. The hungry crew squint at the bright menu board.

A distorted voice booms from the Quickie Food intercom, "Welcome to Quickie Food Unlimited. Would you like to try a Quickie Combo Meal today?"

Kerry places his order from the back seat. "Yeah, uh, I want a steak sandwich, two orders of chimi poppers–"

"Do you want the combo?" asks the intercom.

"*No.*" Kerry shakes his head at the interruption. "Bro." After a pause he continues to rattle off the order. "One steak sandwich, two chimi poppers, a small strawberry shake–"

Denise shouts from the passenger seat, "Are your shakes made with real strawberries?"

"Excuse me?"

"Are the shakes made with real strawberries?"

"Hold on."

Arno groans loudly. "Gawd, I'm hungry."

The voice on the intercom comes back after a moment. "No, they are not made with real strawberries."

"Do you still want it?" Kerry asks Denise. She shrugs her shoulders.

"You can get a large for an additional thirty-five cents," says the intercom voice.

"Bro! *No*. Don't try to up-sell me, you dig?" Kerry threatens belligerently.

"And a burger pocket," Ryan adds.

"Do you want cheese in the pocket?" queries the intercom.

"Whatever."

"Get me one too," says Arno.

"Make that two pockets," corrects Ryan. "You want cheese in your pocket, Denise?"

"I didn't get a pocket."

"She only wants meat in her pocket," Arno says.

"What are you laughing at Kerry? What's so funny?" she asks the guys. "You're all idiots."

"So, we have a Gibbles' style steak sandwich, two orders of world-famous mini chimi poppers, two burger pockets with cheese, and a *small* strawberry shake. Will that be it?"

"Yeah, dipfuck! That's it!" Kerry yells impatiently.

"Okay. Please pull up to the window for your total."

"Ryan, can you spot me a couple bucks?" asks Arno.

"I need to borrow some cash too," says Kerry. "I'll get you back tomorrow."

"You already owe me gas money! I don't have any cash anyway," Ryan says. He looks at Denise expectantly.

"I have a dollar."

* * *

Be Courteous and Be Prompt. Kevin prides himself at getting every order fulfilled to the highest standard of Quickie Food Unlimited's Code of Excellence. The same Code of Excellence that has transcended itself entirely throughout every other faction of his life. Kevin started as a Team Member when he was sixteen and in two years Quickie Food had named him employee of the month a total of eight times and promoted him to Team Leader with a sixty-three cent hourly pay raise.

Living by the Code is what truly made it possible. In that time he has learned the unwritten, but often spoken, third rule of the Code: *Be Courteous, Be Prompt, and Don't-Fuck-Up.*

He doesn't normally work the graveyard shift, but with Vasquez no-showing again, Kevin was called in. He likes to prove his dependability to the higher-ups. *I bet I make DTL in less than a year. Yeah,* he dreams, *Division Team Leader!*

"Maria, you got those poppers ready?" he calls to a middle-aged woman who finishes scooping the fried food into a carton. She plops the carton down the poppers shoot where Kevin adds it to the 'to go' bag.

Kevin checks the itemized receipt as he holds the bag of food out of the drive-up window. "Your total is, uh, fourteen seventy-eight. Need napkins or ketchup?" He jiggles the bag of food, but no one takes it. "Hello?" He tries to keep his impatience hidden by adjusting his glasses, before leaning outside of the window to look into the customer's vehicle.

What Kevin sees shocks him to the core, pimpling his skin in nightmarish fright. Sitting in the driver's seat of an old brown sedan, its skin greenish and desiccant, one side of its mouth decayed in a horrific corpulent smile, is a *zombie! It's finally happened! The living dead!*

At the peak of his horror, the food is ripped out of Kevin's hands by a teen covered in dirt.

"I got it!" celebrates the teen.

Kevin sees the zombie pushed to the middle of the front seat by someone wearing a ski mask and dark brown turtleneck who had apparently been hiding below the steering wheel.

"Kerry, let's go!"

"Hey! You owe fourteen seventy-eight!"

"Eat shit, nerd!" a girl yells from inside the car.

The dirt-covered teen, Kerry, strikes Kevin in the side of the head, knocking his glasses off his face. Kevin falls halfway out the drive-thru window, clawing at Kerry's clothes and trying to grab the food back.

"Get off me, twister!" Kerry beats his way free from Kevin's clutches and hops into the fleeing brown car.

Kevin tries to memorize the license plate, but it is no use without his glasses. They got away. As blood runs from a cut across his forehead and he quivers from the flush of adrenaline, he can only think about one thing. *Corporate's going to be PO'ed!*

MOUTHFUL

THE DEFILER RUMBLES INTO A SEMI-DESERTED
Super Mart UnLTD parking lot as the asphalt for the mega-store is
being sprayed down–sterilized–by a couple workers using industrial
hoses attached to a truck. Ryan parks the Chrysler up away from the
spray and the gang get out, except for Arno, who stays in the car
with an arm around the corpse, finishing his burger pocket.

Denise rolls a chimi popper in her mouth, staring at the human
husk, its lifeless flesh a pallid green-gray, the yellowish light of the
parking lot playing haunting shadows as its skeletal rictus laughs
silently along with Arno. "I can't eat anymore," she says as she spits
her food out and tosses the rest on the ground. "What are we going
to do with that thing now?"

Kerry licks the grease from his fingers and stares longingly
at the edibles Denise threw away. "What do you guys want to do
next?" he asks.

After a brief thoughtful silence, Denise says, "We could go
somewhere and have a coffee?"

"That's *lame*," states Ryan.

"Well everything else closed at ten!"

"Where's your camera?" Kerry asks Ryan. "I want to get a picture for the yearbook."

"I didn't bring it."

"Bro! I said to get it!"

"That's how people get caught, Klingon," Ryan says. "Leaving evidence like that is amateur."

"You're being Captain Un-fun," Kerry says.

Arno abruptly lets out a girlish scream from inside the car, grabbing the mild attention from everybody.

"What's wrong with you?" asks Ryan.

Arno hops out of the car and dances around in hysterics. "This guy's package's shriveled up! Damn completely!" he laughs. "Looks like a gross, burnt, dried-up piece of sausage."

"Fag," Kerry slurs.

Denise pushes past Arno to see for herself. "Maybe he was your real father?"

Arno splutters at Denise's verbal attack. "Maybe you want to suck this one, too!"

Kerry slaps Arno across the face, hard, sending the half-chewed burger pocket flying from Arno's mouth. "I already told you once, mother!"

Ryan just watches his friends attack each other in an exchange of insults and fists while consuming the last morsel of his burger pocket with cheese. *Everything here is lame.*

* * *

Lennox stares at the wooden skeleton of one of the future homes in Everdale's Paloma Estates, concentrating hard on anything besides his friend Rollo sitting next to him, or Rollo's little brother Doyle lying prone on his other side. He gives himself mental congratulations for being able to engineer his truck into this position by the rock wall. After all, his ride is sitting on 40-inch bog tires.

Rollo let's out a long sigh and a small laugh before hopping off the tailgate. "I'm done."

"Shut up," Doyle groans through pursed lips, squeezing his eyes shut and running his hand through his bowl-haircut.

Lennox answers an incoming call on his cellular phone while at the same time trying to refocus his attention, deciding to stare at a spot in his truck bed where the white paint has chipped away.

Rollo stands next to the truck cab, wiping his genitals clean. "I'm glad you brought your sweatshirt, Doyle."

Doyle shakes his head without responding.

"I wouldn't *be* at a place that's not cool," Lennox tells the caller breathlessly, trying to hide a climactic gasp. He rolls off the truck bed and zips his fly. "I might stop by."

"Think they got any copper wire around here?" Rollo asks.

Lennox shrugs, then snaps his phone closed. "Are you done yet?" he calls to Doyle.

"He's goin' soft," rasps a voice from between Doyle's legs.

Lennox looks over at the meth-head standing on the wall and servicing Doyle. Doyle is staring at him with a big foolish grin on his face, trying to make eye contact.

"What is he doing?" Rollo asks.

The woman sputters, coughing up a mouthful of liquid. She loses her balance and falls to the dirt, getting sprayed by Doyle. Laughing, Doyle jumps off the bed, pulling up his pants, and races into the truck.

"You li'l pecker!" the haggard meretrix screams, her entire front drenched with urine.

Rollo cackles as he pulls himself into the giant truck.

"She already smelled like piss anyway," Doyle says.

Lennox starts up his ride. "Let's get out of here."

"Give me my *money!*" the disgruntled muleskinner demands, limping up from the ground and slapping on the back of the truck. "Where you think you goin'?"

Lennox's rage flares and he jams the door open, cracking the angry old bat in the face. She falls to her knees sniveling, and whimpers at the blood gushing from her nose. "Don't *ever, eeever,* touch my truck!" He curses and grabs a couple large bills from his center console, tossing them out the window at her before hitting the gas.

Gravel kicks up on the despicable good-for-nothing as the trio speed out of the construction area. By the time they hit the main roads, Lennox feels his anger subside.

"That was the funniest shit," Rollo congratulates his brother.

"I think she swallowed some of that!"

Lennox chuckles while listening to his friends relive the past five minutes, and lets out a large sigh as he watches a police cruiser turn onto the interstate. It seems nearly every car on the streets at this time of night is a cop. With scorn, he gestures out the window to a brown four-door sedan double-parked under a street lamp at Super Mart. "Look at this trash."

"It looks like they are arguing or something," Rollo says, studying the scene. " I think it's Kerry and his slutty girlfriend Denise."

"I bet that retard Arno's with 'em too," Doyle says from the backseat.

"That pussy fruitcake?" says Rollo. "He's a god damn double-decker douche!"

"A total double-decker," Doyle agrees.

"Let's roll 'em!"

"We'll just see what's going on," Lennox says.

* * *

The sound of an approaching engine hits Ryan's ears, triggering his internal alarm. "Shit!" He looks at the corpse in his car, then at Arno who is nearest. "Arno, hide Jeffrey!"

"Jeffrey?" Arno's confusion vanishes in the next instant. He whips around, panic stricken by the seized merchandise in the backseat. "With what? There isn't anything!"

"Use your shirt," recommends Kerry.

Denise looks ready to run off. "Is it the cops?"

Arno hastily pulls off his shirt and drapes it over the corpse's head as a giant vehicle pulls up shining its high beams.

Ryan attempts to shield his eyes with his fingers and make out who the newcomer is. He relaxes a little when he recognizes the white Chevy 2500 HD extended cab 4-wheel drive with a giant lift, that ramps over a grassy median and enters the Super Mart UnLTD parking area. *It's just that asshole Lennox.*

"Hey chicken shits," Lennox calls, leaning his head out of the window and revving the huge Chevy in an attempted show of dominance.

"Your truck sounds like squirting diarrhea," Ryan says as he follows Kerry to the driver side of the lifted truck. "You might want to check your compression."

"Lick my onions, numbnuts," Lennox responds. "Don't act like you know anything about cars, driving that choadster."

"Not all of us have mommy and daddy to pay our way," Kerry says. "You're just a spoiled bitch."

Lennox struggles to turn his scowl into a smirk. "What are you scabs doin'?"

"Just kickin' around," Ryan says. "What's it to you?"

"Ain't shit to me."

Rollo recoils sourly when he sees Arno. "The fat one ate his shirt."

"Oh yeah look!" Doyle squeals. "Look at those nipples!"

"See something you like?" taunts Arno, patting his exposed belly.

"Your goddamn gunt is making me nauseous." Rollo dry heaves out the window.

"Arno's making Rollo gag again." Kerry says.

"Balls deep!" Ryan adds.

"Screw you, pissants!" Rollo cries.

Ryan and his friends laugh as Rollo's face darkens.

Lennox rolls his eyes. "You gays check out that party on Forty-third?" he wonders aloud.

"Party?" Arno perks up. "Whose party?"

Lennox grins at his passengers as if they share a secret.

Ryan can feel his face get hot at Lennox's show of arrogance. "What are you cappers smiling at?"

"Nothing, Ryan," Lennox answers smugly. "It's usual that slags like you are just hanging out with nothing to do." Lennox sighs. "It's usual. Sad really. Nobody likes you."

"And people like *you*?" Ryan throws back, temper unleashed.

"Why wouldn't they?"

"You reek like nutsack."

"That's because I have one."

"On your chin!"

Arno hawks up a giant olive-green loogie and spits it high in a big arc to land onto the hood of Lennox's shiny truck. Everyone just stares at the slimy ooze for a tense moment; it's an act of aggression that may have crossed the line.

A war is taking place behind Lennox's eyes. "Well...I see," he says icily. "I was going to tell you about this party, but since your cum stain friend here spit on my truck, you can eat my dick!"

"Screw your party."

Lennox stares murder at Ryan and Kerry, but winks at Denise. "See you later, Denise."

Denise responds with a confused wave as Lennox races away, with Doyle hanging out the passenger window cursing at Ryan and crew.

The gang watch the Chevy obliterate a stop sign as it hops onto the main road and out of sight.

"Man...those guys are so nothin'," Kerry struggles for the words, "such *nobodies*."

"Arno, you're such an a-hole," Denise says with a laugh.

Arno tries to hide a blush behind a question. "So what do you... uh...think?"

Ryan looks at the half covered body in his car. "Do you guys want to go to a party?"

5

PAT'S PARENTS DON'T MIND IF HE HAS A FEW FRIENDS over while they're gone on international sightseeing holidays. They feel that socializing is a healthy and necessary aspect of proper character growth. Anyway, Patrick wouldn't be caught dead as third wheel to another of their old fart journeys–not since he grew his first pube. *Where did they go again? Milan? Madrid?*

Under dancing candlelight, Pat ostentatiously studies himself in the vanity mirror set in the corner of his parents' master bedroom. He likes how the flickering light plays across his body, making his skin appear smoother and giving his facial features a dangerous look. He cranes his neck to pose with his new bad-boy earring and unties his father's robe from his waist to let it hang open casually. Pat wants the luscious raven-haired girl sitting on the king bed to see how glorious his stuff is.

It's a little game he likes. In his domain, his playing field, he makes the rules of this sport of seduction. He knows that kids need a place to do drugs, drink, have sex, and whatever, so Pat does the kind thing and offers his house as a teenage hangout. And what does Pat get in return?

"You have a nice place," the raven-haired girl comments. "Is this the end of the tour?" She sips from her Blackberry Bartles & Jaymes like she's a film noir starlet, but coming off a little like a girl playing with mommy's make-up.

Pat is deciding how to make his next move when he hears the thumping beat from the new single 'Show You Mine' by Leila coming from downstairs. *I told those twits not so loud. They're gonna get the cops called!*

"Oh shit!" The raven-haired girl drops her drink in her lap, splashing some of the wine cooler onto the bed. She groans mostly at the loss of her beverage rather than getting it on the silk sheets.

Stupid tramp! Pat comes to the girl's aid to survey the damage. "Party foul," Pat says feebly, trying to not let the mood be broken. He was planning on staining the sheets anyway. "Oh look, you got some on your shirt, too," he says with loss. "Oh…and your pants."

"Ew, it's all sticky."

"I guess you better take your shirt off," Pat says slyly.

The raven-haired girl puts her film noir act back in place and laughs airily at Pat's comment. She looks at him with smoky, alluring eyes. Pat's stomach tightens in anticipation and he breathes her in. *She smells like blueberry muffins.* The girl unbuttons her blouse slowly, like she is performing for a movie camera and this is an important moment, with all eyes on her. Pat feels a shift in the game, like he has now become the prey in this sport of seduction. It's as if the girl is a lion cub awkwardly learning to hunt, but with a predator's natural instincts and ability.

"You are…like an *angel*," Pat encourages.

The girl unsnaps her bra, sliding it down to reveal her lovely breasts. Pat can barely breathe. He reaches his hands out to cup them, but is jolted by a large crash from downstairs. *What the bloody hell?!* Pat's captivation by the girl's .delicates is rudely disturbed with another crash coming from the lower rooms, now accompanied with some yelling.

* * *

"Mess him up baby!" Denise is cheering Kerry who is locked in some sort of clumsy wrestling struggle with an out-of-breath Rollo. Arno lies over a smashed coffee table groaning in pain and clutching his ribs.

"You're about to die, Ryan, you pussy!" Doyle screams from behind Lennox's shoulder. Lennox and Ryan are squaring off in a pit made of drinking teens that fill the living room of whoever's house this is. The drunken teens encircling them cheer and laugh. Some of the crowd try to dismiss the hoopla as immature and not worth their attention, attempting to carry on with their conversations and drinking games.

Ryan swings a forty-ounce like a monkey with a stick as Lennox and Doyle split to mount an attack from opposite sides.

"Why are you here, you piece of shit?" spits Lennox. "You're unwanted."

Doyle feints at Ryan, Ryan cracks him across the temple with the bottle; it bounces out of his hand without breaking, but sends Doyle yelping in pain. Lennox rushes Ryan and knees him in the back, heaving Ryan into an onlooker and throwing them both into the wall in a tumbling splash of jungle juice and limbs.

"Get off me you stupid jerk!" The unfortunate partier tries to push Ryan away, but Lennox has pounced and is attempting to choke Ryan out from behind. People who started out as cheerleaders are now trying to break the scuffle apart, while the ones that were trying to ignore the spectacle are now drawn into it.

BANG!

The entire party seizes in shock from the abrupt gunshot. A man with slicked-back hair, wearing a silk robe and holding a pistol, stands in the middle of the curving staircase that leads to the bedrooms upstairs. "What the hell is this?" he demands in a boiling fury, his single earring dangling wildly. "This is my house, and my party." He gestures the gun at Kerry and Rollo who are panting from their battle. "Who are you?" He sees Arno getting up from the ruined furniture and Lennox and Ryan gathering themselves. "I didn't invite any of you tools."

"Oh this is your place, huh?" Kerry asks with an edge to his voice. "Are you threatening me with that piece?"

"I want you all to leave. Everyone, party is *over.*"

"You candy-assed fairy," says Kerry.

The guy chambers a round in his gun then points it at Kerry. "Leave."

Kerry mad-dogs the man on the staircase. "Oh, you gonna shoot me?"

A piercing shriek comes from the front yard, followed a second later by someone from outside shouting 'Oh my god!' in complete terror.

* * *

The whole party empties into the front of the house where a young couple has just arrived from a waiting taxi. The guy is hugging his girlfriend—who is sobbing uncontrollably and looking about to throw-up.

The cabbie is evidently waiting for them to pay for his services. "Hey stupid! Don't you little bastards try and stiff me!"

"That guy's dead," the girl groans, pointing at a shadowy figure on the stoop, who appears to be relaxing next to a bottle of brew. On closer examination, it becomes clearer that the immobile shadow is the corpse of a young man whose remains have been puppeteered into a 'chill' position. The display has attracted a mass of people pointing and talking amongst themselves. Some of the partiers laugh while most are stunned or confused.

"I don't give a shit, stupid!" the cabbie goes on yelling. "You pay me or I'll break your fingers! One, two, three, forever!"

The boy consoling the girl pulls out his wallet to handle the wired cab driver.

"Holy shit," Doyle utters as he exits the house and spots the root of excitement. He tenderly probes the purple and black lump forming on his head while searching for his friends among the crowd.

"Everybody calm down," instructs Arno, gingerly gathering up the dead body. "He's with us. Nothing to worry about."

"Is that real?" someone asks.

"It's not over between us!" Lennox warns ominously before he charges away with Rollo and Doyle right behind.

"Let's get out of here," says Kerry. "This party is toast."

Ryan is way ahead, already outside of the milling partiers and walking back to his car.

"Hey kid!" the cabbie yells at Arno. "Where did you get that?"

"Up yours," is Arno's answer.

The cabbie reels with the disrespectful reply. "Up mine? Nobody tells Fancy Jack Clancy up his, see? You disgusting, *dis*figured, *dis*grace!"

"I gave you a fifty," says the boy who paid the cab fare. "Who the hell are you!?" screams the cabby. "You're nobody sucker! See?" The cabby looks back toward Arno who had really ticked him off, but he has seemingly disappeared.

"Where's my change?" the boy asks.

"What do you mean where's your change, huh?" Fancy Jack puts his cab in drive. "You see what happened here, stupid?" He takes off in a dangerous apoplexy.

"WHAT DID THAT ASSHOLE HIT ME WITH?" ARNO massages the back of his head, letting the wind coming in through the passenger side window of The Defiler cool his alcohol-induced warmth.

Ryan coasts the sedan to a stop at another empty intersection. "His fist I think." He readjusts the rearview away from the corpse's lifeless stare from the backseat to an equally nauseating sight of Kerry and Denise making-out.

"Kerry, where's that bottle?" Arno asks, turning around in his seat to deliver his question directly.

Kerry sees his friends watching him suck face with his girlfriend, but doesn't stop. He moans loudly while gliding his hand across Denise's chest. He gives it a squeeze and then pulls down Denise's shirt, exposing her pert areola.

"Wha–!?" Denise realizes what is happening and slaps Kerry across the face. "You *a*-holes!" she snarls as she pulls her shirt back up.

"Nice titties, Denise."

The boys laugh, but Denise turns red. "Holy shit, Arno! Is that your breath? It smells like freaking *poop!*"

Arno is briefly stunned by Denise's words. "...poop?" The guys just laugh harder while Denise huddles in on herself, shaking her head.

Ryan wipes the laughter-tears from his eyes to examine the early model Sentra that has stopped alongside The Defiler. He can't see the driver due to its thickly tinted windows, but he notices the Sentra has a spare donut tire on the front passenger side. *Time for some real fun.* Ryan gives his car some gas while holding his left foot on the brake.

"Yeah, boy!" shouts Arno. "You gonna drag 'im?"

Ryan squeezes the steering wheel and watches the blinking 'Don't Walk' sign from the perpendicular street. He revs the engine again, louder, but there is no visible sign that the Sentra noticed.

"You're going down!" Kerry yells out the window.

The light turns green, Ryan slams the gas, and both cars smoke off the starting line. Ryan laughs in excitement as his friends cheer him on. The thrill of the race burns hotly through Ryan and his heart pumps fire through his system to the surging beat of the mechanized animal in his grip. The Newport and Sentra are neck and neck. Forty–Fifty–Sixty miles an hour.

"Come on, Ryan!"

"Faster!"

"Go! Go! Go!"

"He's going to beat you!"

In a burst, the Sentra pulls in front, quickly outdistancing the Newport, and speeds through the yellow light of the next intersection. Ryan judges his distance to the changing light and locks up his brakes. Arno squawks, and the sedan fishtails into the intersection as the light turns red.

Kerry and Denise snicker to each other as Ryan angrily reverses behind the crosswalk.

"Man," jeers Denise, "you suck."

"Majorly," adds Kerry.

Ryan scans the passengers in the car, three living, one not. He pounds the steering wheel, livid at his defeat. "I got too much dead weight in this car!"

Kerry pats the corpse. "Hey, it's not your fault, buddy."

"I was talking about you fuckshits," Ryan growls.

Green light and Ryan slowly continues on, gnashing his teeth. *Maybe I need a larger engine in this thing?*

"Hey!" Arno calls out the window. "Yo!" He has apparently spotted someone he knows at the late night Mexican restaurant Super Tacos UnLTD. "Stop real quick," he says to Ryan.

The Defiler's tires whine painfully, rubbing against the curb as Ryan pulls the car over.

"What the hell, Arno?" demands Kerry.

Arno jumps out of the car and approaches a couple sitting on the hood of an old El Camino.

"Ryan, what's he doing?"

"I don't know."

"Aw, it's just Abby," Denise says, watching Arno start to get into it with the couple. "Who's that guy she's with?" She sounds amused. "That stupid *whore*."

"Screw this." Ryan hits the gas.

"You're leaving Arno," Kerry points out.

"Oops."

The crew continue wordlessly and without objective. The night sky is beginning to brighten. After a mile or so, Kerry interrupts the awkward silence.

"Hey bro, drop me and Denise off at her house, okay?"

"We have to do something with him first." Ryan gestures to the corpse.

"We don't give a shit!" Denise screeches. "Drop us off!"

"Screw you!"

"Just throw it in a dumpster somewhere," says Kerry.

"You two are coming with me."

"Come on, you can't do it alone?"

"I'm not your patsy!"

"Just take us *home!*" hollers Denise. "Do it yourself!"

Ryan crushes the brake pedal under his foot, stopping the car in a violent spasm. "I'm not taking you fucktards anywhere," he growls. "Get out!"

"Are you kidding me?"

Ryan reaches over and opens the rear passenger door. "Both of you, out of my car."

Kerry bails out of the car and says, "You're such a twink."

"You *nut* bag!" mutters Denise.

Ryan hits the gas before Denise can get completely clear, causing her to fall to the pavement.

"Watch it!" she yells after him.

He drifts a one-eighty and punches The Defiler directly at his friends. Kerry pulls a screaming Denise inches out of harm's way and both tumble to the ground.

Ryan howls like a maniac, but the corpse doesn't say anything.

7

WHAT DO I DO WITH THIS CORPSE? RYAN NOTICES that the sky has turned a deep blue. He sees a few more cars on the road along with a police patrol. Early birds will be out starting their day soon. He yawns widely. The excitement of the night and the late hour has worn him out. *Maybe I can just throw it on the side of the road.*

Ryan looks at his silent passenger. *I should probably bring it back to the cemetery. Kerry leaves me with this shit!? He's such a–*

BEEP! BEEP!

Ryan is startled by an angry motorist he almost ran into at a stop sign he didn't see. The motorist drives though the intersection slowly, shaking his head at Ryan. Ryan just puts up his hands and shrugs. *I'm dozing off and it's getting bright out here. I'll probably make an amateurish mistake and get caught dumping this biohazard. There are cameras everywhere.*

"Screw it," Ryan says to the corpse. "You're not in any hurry are you?"

* * *

Ryan fumbles the door open to his filthy bedroom, carries the corpse in, and sets it down on a chair in the corner. Ryan's room is like most teenage boys' rooms, decorated with posters of cars and women, random nameless junk, and messed up with strewn clothes, food wrappers and other trash. He has left the TV on like he always does. He usually keeps it at a low volume because he never really watches it. He just likes the glow.

"In America," comes a voice from the TV at the level of a whisper, "the common ground is rust, wheat and beige; not red, white or blue."

"What do you mean by that, Councilmember?"

"I mean that to get along in America you have to conform to the middle. You have to find a common ground with so many diverse cultures. In my experience, it doesn't necessarily *pay* to be different. It pays to be part of the team."

"I still fail to see the connection."

"To be part of a team," the voice drones on, "to be a real team player, you must conform to the team. And for everyone to get along within a diverse team, I feel that they must limit their conflicting opinions that cause emotional strain on each other. If I were to put a color to limited emotion, I would color it brown."

"Thank you, Councilmember Geier. *Rust, Wheat, and Beige* on bookshelves today. Coming up next..."

Ryan snarls at the morning news that is already on for the sad bastards just waking up. Everyone on the TV seems so happy and this always pisses Ryan off. *No one can be that happy this early and all the time. They're so full of shit.* Ryan pulls out a couple coins from his pocket and sets them on the TV. *I'm sick of having no god damn money. Maybe I'll get a job tomorrow.* He crashes on his unmade bed without bothering to undress and tries to put his financial situation and the news anchors' repulsive phony act out of his mind.

The Defiler is screaming so fast down the highway it leaves a trail of fire in its wake. Ryan urges his car faster, drunk on the speed and power. He spots Doyle standing in the middle of the road in a Karate pose. Ryan presses the gas to the floor and screams in unison with the roaring motor as he hits Doyle dead on, exploding him into a fine red mist.

"Yee-ha! Ya got 'im!" Arno is in the passenger seat having a hell of a time, wearing a shirt made out of dollar bills. "Look, it's Denise." Arno points out Denise sitting at a bus stop wearing nothing but thong panties.

"Take me home, Ryan," she whimpers. "I'm *so* horny."

Ryan zooms by, and she bursts into flames.

"Oh man, she's hot." Arno rolls down the window. "I'm hot, too. Aren't you hot?" Arno's face starts sizzling.

"Roll up the window!" yells Ryan.

The skin on Arno's face melts away, revealing the rancid decrepitude of Jeffrey The Corpse.

"Faster!"

Sweat drips down Ryan's face and he feels like he might be melting, too. He stomps on the brakes with both feet, but the car goes faster. He can't control it. Everything around him is a blur, spinning into fiery annihilation. His face starts to boil. The car transforms into a blaze and shoots into the sky like a comet, going so fast his eyes pop. The force tears his flesh apart to dissolve behind him in tendrils of skin flaps. Ryan has never felt more alive.

HOLES

DETECTIVE MCCREADY COMBS HIS MUSTACHE WITH his fingers, eyeing the hole in the ground like a hunk of fouled cheese that he was debating whether to toss, or salvage and make into quesadillas. He sighs and wishes he were back in his warm cozy bed and in his warm young wife, rather than at Everdale City Cemetery looking at a hole. *It's too early in the morning for quesadillas.*

"Detective McCready." A lanky man in uniform, with a nametag that reads 'SAPPS', approaches the detective.

"What you got, Pyle?"

"Well, the caretaker says he ain't seen anythin' and there is no video surveillance."

Detective McCready doesn't respond. Sapps annoys McCready, and not just for the twangy accent. He doesn't even know why Sapps is there. *Sapps is a useless yes-man with no ability for independent thought.* McCready smirks to himself. Sapps' nickname at the station is 'Pyle', but not for Gomer Pyle like he thinks–or not only–it's also for 'pile of shit' because that's what he has for brains. Of course Sapps has no idea about this. McCready's silence prompts Sapps to continue.

37

"And well, the caretaker–nice guy–says he hasn't heard of any such *ghoulishness* happenin' in this county in all his years workin' here. Says this is a *bolt from the blue*." Sapps laughs to himself at the expression.

"How long has he worked here?"

The question seems to stun Sapps. "Hm, well, I don't know. The man is pretty old though."

McCready rubs his eyes and gestures to the unearthed grave. "The person who was in this grave had died the same date as today, Pyle," Detective McCready says. "Only so many years ago. What do you make of that?"

"Somethin' to do with satanic rituals, I guess." Sapps itches his scalp. "I don't follow it myself."

"Satanism? What leads you to believe this was done by... what?...a cult of some sort?"

Sapps nods. "Why else would anyone dig up a dead body? Unless you were gonna use it in some sorta spell-casting necro orgy ritual?"

Detective McCready reluctantly agrees–to an extent. *No one is going to dig up a dead person for any decent reason.* Detective McCready was not aware of any satanic cults in Everdale. The thought of a satanic cult in Everdale seems like a silly fantasy, but you never know. He'll have to round up the usual suspects.

"Excuse me, sir?" Sapps addresses a man of great mystique, who is approaching the gravesite.

McCready instinctively feels threatened by this newly arrived man, but his curiosity and professionalism overwhelm any feeling of danger, just barely. *Who the hell is this guy?* McCready observes the tall foreboding man. His skin is tightly stretched over a gaunt unreadable face and hairless scalp, giving the impression of a skeleton, which is only enhanced by the fact his eyes are veiled behind dark sunglasses.

The skeletal man's left ear is almost completely missing–as if ripped or chewed off–and he is cloaked from head to foot in bereavement black; save for grey lettering on his jacket, which reads 'Live Good' above a creepy skull design and 'Die Great' below.

The detective notes the paltry fistful of sanguine poppies and a brown bag that the man clutches in his bony right hand where the charcoal sleeve has pulled back enough to reveal the green, blue, and yellow tattoos that wrap around his forearm in soft designs and travel up toward his elbow like nymphs playing in watery vines.

"We are conductin' an investigation here. I'm goin' to have to ask you to leave." Sapps fails to sound commanding.

The grim man pays no attention to Sapps, but rather, considers the crime scene. He snaps the police tape surrounding the violated gravesite with his sinewy left hand that is covered in sharp tattoo designs colored red, orange, purple, like screaming souls drowning in flowing blood and burning in razor fire.

Sapps reaches for the man. "Hey pal-"

The intimidating man doesn't move, but only seems to tense up, like an animal ready to attack, and Sapps' words trail off, his hand freezing mid-air.

McCready chortles nervously. "Just let him in there, Pyle. Won't harm anything."

Sapps lets his hand fall to his side without touching the man, and watches dimly as the man dressed in black kneels at the unearthed grave.

McCready also takes note of the confident fluid movements of this stranger. *This is indeed a dangerous man.* He watches him lay the flowers down and pick up a piece of the broken burial box. The casket is still in the hole, smashed open. "Are you friend or family?" McCready asks.

The man makes no reply. Instead, he tosses the piece of concrete into the hole with a light clatter.

"Do you know of anyone that might have done this? Maybe knew your friend?" McCready thinks he sees the man shake his head slightly. It could be a response to his question, or not.

"You better answer us!" threatens Sapps. "We can do this the easy way or—"

"*Quiet* your *drivel!*" the man cuts, with a voice as tough as carving steel.

The man in black picks a severed plaster cherub head out of some of the unearthed dirt. Sapps and McCready watch in awe as the specter-like man inspects the babyish features he holds gently in his bony right hand, then touches it to his lips like a kiss, before squeezing it and crushing it into dust, letting the cool wind carry away the ashes.

"They were drinking," the man mumbles. "Beer. Cheap beer."

"Wow," remarks Sapps. "You got all that from a little angel head?"

The man turns in his crouch toward Sapps with the manner of a venomous snake. He bares his teeth in a hissing snarl and looks Sapps dead in the eye. The hairs on McCready's neck stand up at the deep-throated growl coming from the unnerving man. Sapps steps back defensively and jumps when the man suddenly juts out his left arm and barks, "There's a can right over there!"

Sapps' eyes follow the man's arm to where he points to an empty tall can laying nearby in the grass. He tries to hide his embarrassment at showing fear by rubbing his chin thoughtfully.

The skeletal man walks over to the discarded can, picks it up, and inspects it. "Jalisco's. Ninety-nine cents," he grumbles, pointing out a pink price sticker on the can.

"Well mister…" McCready fishes for the man's name with no success. "I want you to know that we are *fully* dedicated to recovering the remains of the departed. You can be confident that whoever did this heinous act will be caught and properly punished to the maximum extent of the law." The detective swallows despite himself as the strange man turns his dark impenetrable gaze his way. *This guy is insane!*

The man dressed in blackness stands up, tosses the beer can to the ground, and turns to go the way he came. "Fuck your law."

JALISCO'S MINI-MART IS A SMALL BRICK BUILDING where the local illegals come to cash their checks and buy booze. The owner of the place, 'Old Man' Jalisco, a sun-leathered fragile-looking man of innumerable years, lives alone in an adjacent apartment out back.

It is early afternoon in the small dirt parking area for the convenience store, and Ryan is out there scrounging for change in The Defiler's ashtray. He fumbles around slowly, his motor skills awkward and strained due to the fact that he just rolled out of bed. Ryan has discarded the turtleneck from the previous night in favor of more casual wear; however, he still dons the fingerless workout gloves.

At this time of day, Jalisco's doesn't have much business. The usual clientele normally don't start to come around until after work hours. There are a few lurkers that pretty much hang outside the place all day though. Like Wanda, a lady emaciated beyond reason with rotten teeth and stringy hair; forty years old going on eighty, the whites of her eyes aged to yellow from all the crack, and her clothes were rags before she found them. She's a lurker. Frequently hanging around outside Jalisco's asking for change.

One time, Ryan saw her and a young construction worker enter the outdoor washroom together and they didn't come out for about fifteen minutes. Ryan thinks Wanda is what some refer to as a lot lizard. A prostitute. Today, Wanda's got toilet paper stuffed in one nostril and is lazily sunning herself on the sidewalk outside Jalisco's door.

Once Ryan is satisfied with the weight of coins in his hand, he gets out of his car and locks the door. *You can't trust any of these creepsters around here.* Ryan returns Wanda's greeting with a nod before entering the store.

He walks past the extremely old storeowner behind the register who is sitting hunched over, practically motionless, on a wooden stool. As usual, a small boombox behind the counter adds music full of horns and accordions into the atmosphere.

"*Hola*, Mister Jalisco," Ryan greets. "How are you today, sir?"

Mr. Jalisco comes out of his daze to utter something unintelligible then returns to staring into nothing.

Ryan bypasses the snack food, goes directly to the beer cooler and grabs a couple of tall cans. He lazily scuttles around the aisles, browsing for something interesting before stopping to inspect a bulletin board full of advertisements, rentals, and for sales. He cracks one of the beers open and takes a long drink, moaning with complete refreshment. *It is good to start out the day with your carbs for breakfast.* Ryan believes he heard that advice somewhere. A handwritten notice on the board catches his eye. It reads:

WANT 2 MAKE TONS OF CASH?
Call 999-5150
Join The Team! Today!

The posting has individual sections to tear off with the number. Ryan tries to take just one, but tears half the page off. He puts the paper in his pocket and goes up and sets the beers on the checkout counter.

"Anything else?" the old clerk mutters.

"This is it."

"ID."

"Wait a second. Is that the new issue of 'CREASE'?" Ryan points to the small rack of smut mags on the ground behind Mr. Jalisco. "Whoa, Whoa! Come on, right there." Ryan vehemently directs Mr. Jalisco's attention to the February issue of CREASE, one of the more hardcore rags. This month's cover is graced by the multi-talented artist Leila Caverns. *Music, movies, and more. Is there anything she can't do?* A full erotic exposé is promised within the glorious glossy pages.

It takes what seems like an eternity for Mr. Jalisco to make his way off his seat and to the adult rack. While Mr. Jalisco's back is turned, Ryan takes the opportunity to snag a handful of mini liquor bottles that are in a large bowl next to the register and stuff them in his pockets. Mr. Jalisco eventually returns with the magazine on the counter.

"Anything else?" Mr. Jalisco asks tiredly.

"I think this will do it," says Ryan. He peels open the issue of CREASE, getting an eyeful of gorgeous Leila. "Holy smokes!"

"ID please."

"Yeah, absolutely." Ryan pulls out his Velcro wallet and tears it open to an identification card of one Alphonzo Casañas and hands it to Mr. Jalisco. Ryan sips from the open beer while studying the little delicate hairs covering Leila's flawless skin.

Mr. Jalisco finishes examining Alphonzo's ID and hands it back to Ryan satisfied. He begins to calculate the merchandise by hand with a pencil and pad of paper, his hand trembling as he tallies up the items.

"You know what?" Ryan drawls. "I already have this one." He drops the magazine on the counter along with his handful of collected change, mostly copper, which scatters everywhere. "You can keep it."

Mr. Jalisco isn't paying any mind to what Ryan is saying. He is too busy counting the coins that Ryan dumped on the counter.

Ryan slams the rest of his open beer with a verbal expression of satisfaction. "Do you have a trash bucket back there, Mr. Jalisco?" Ryan asks, leaning over the counter. "Oh sure you do." He tosses the empty can, which clatters on the floor behind the register, and leaves Mr. Jalisco counting the change.

SAMMY'S AUTO UNLTD, A CORPORATE AUTO PARTS chain with a cartoonish Uncle Sam caricature as a mascot, operates just down the avenue from Jalisco's Mini-Mart, which makes it accommodating for Ryan. Despite the slogan that 'Sammy's Wants You! …To Save!', Ryan has never seen any real difference in price when compared with U.S. Auto down the street. *They both probably have the same supplier.*

Ryan walks the aisles with his hands full of performance-enhancing products like fuel additive and filters; things he needs for The Defiler after the humiliating defeat last night. His head throbs as the current chart topper 'Show You Mine' buzzing over the PA system is interrupted every now and then by sales promos; first in English, then Spanish.

He's busy searching for the right oil weight when a shiny object stops him dead in his tracks. It's a glistening, brand-new, giant blower engine on display. He stares at the sexiness of its curves, captivated by the untainted cleanliness and craftsmanship that promises maximum muscle. *This is just what I need!* He licks his lips at a handwritten sign that prices the supercharged engine at twenty-percent off. *It might as well be a million bucks.*

"Want a little extra get-up-and-go? Ask one of our team members about our many different sparkplugs available," suggests a pre-recorded voice over the public announcement system. "Remember to buckle up! We value your patronage, *and* your safety."

As the message repeats in Spanish, Ryan pries himself away from the object of consumer desire and takes his merchandise to the checkout. Stationed behind the counter is a leathery woman sporting feathered hair, who is currently busy using her Sammy's polo shirt to dab at a grease stain dribbled on her khakis. Ryan stands there staring until she acknowledges his existence.

"Find everything okay, hun?" she croaks between her brown smoker's teeth.

"Hey, um, that engine," Ryan points to the display he was admiring, "do you think it would fit in my car out there?"

The clerk cranes her neck to look over Ryan's heather brown 1980 Chrysler Newport.

"That junker?" She sounds offended. She gives herself a shake after seeing Ryan's unsatisfied expression, seemingly to remind herself of Team Sammy's credo, and tries to concentrate on being helpful. "Hmmm…" She studies the engine for a brief moment before shrugging her shoulders and offering her professional advice. "Sure. Why not?"

Ryan just looks at her with disgust.

"What year is it?" she asks, still pretending to be constructive.

"Are you guys hiring?"

"No."

"Are you the manager?"

"*No*, I'm *not*." Shaking her head, the lady fishes out a form attached to a clipboard from under the counter. "The Career Kiosk is on the fritz, so if you want to apply, you're going to have to do this the old way. Fill this out and bring it back if you like. I'm out of the English though."

Ryan looks over the application, but can't decipher it because it's written in Spanish. "Screw that."

11

THE INDEPENDENCE HIGH PARKING LOT, WHERE
the students are currently returning from lunch break, is a dangerous
place due to highly inexperienced drivers trying to race back to class
before the tardy buzzer. Ryan scopes out the hot freshman meat as
he mixes into the heavy traffic. A redhead and a brunette with braces
walk by as if he was just background scenery.

"I know you see me," Ryan says, but they continue on as if
they don't. He spots Arno walking by himself and pulls up alongside
him. "Yo, fat ass!"

"Ryan!" Arno hails. "What happened to you last night, fool?"

"What's going on?"

Arno peers around. "Not much. You got any suds?" He reaches
into the car and pops open the glove compartment. A tall can of
beer rolls out, but Ryan quickly closes it back into the compartment.
Arno acts like he was slapped. "What the hell, Goldfarb? Don't be
getting stingy."

"Hold on, leech." Ryan digs in his pocket and fishes out a
couple mini bottles of liquor and offers them to Arno. "Here. Have
a ball or two."

Arno accepts the bottles, snaps one open, swallows its contents, and drops the empty container on the ground. "What did you end up doing with Johnny?" he asks Ryan.

"What the hell is Johnny?" Ryan asks, but after a second it clicks. "Oh you mean Jeffrey, right?"

"What are you doing here shit face?" Kerry asks as he and Denise walk up on the passenger side holding hands. Denise is coughing into her fist like she just got out of a burning building.

Ryan senses he might be stopped awhile and sets The Defiler into park to let the engine idle slower and then says to his friend, "Screw you."

Kerry takes a lean on Ryan's Chrysler. "Did you do anything else last night? Besides go stroke yourself?"

"I just did my own thing."

"What an aristocrat," Denise chokes. The effort to speak appears to have dislodged something in her throat, making her loudly hack up some phlegm. She drools it on the ground, repulsing everyone around.

"What's wrong with you?" Ryan asks Denise.

"You're an a-hole. That's what's wrong with me." She gives Kerry a sloppy kiss. "Alright baby, I'm going to class." She makes a face at Ryan and leaves sounding like she's got a kazoo in her chest.

Kerry waits until Denise is out of earshot. "So what's up tonight? Want to sneak into the Bush Company again? Get a bush dive?" He punches his palm and says in remembrance, "Oh wait, I'm busted. Nevermind."

"Let's knife some old people," Arno puts in. He pantomimes a kidney thrust for theatrical argument.

"I might have to skip it," Ryan says. "I'm gonna do some more job hunting I think."

"Oh yeah? I'm thinking about coming to the school social tomorrow night, and selling the freshman some herbal ecstasy," states Kerry.

"Sounds like some more *bull*shit."

"What's wrong with you? Is your twat still sore from last night?"

"It's nothing," Ryan says sourly. "Just next time you have another brilliant scheme that requires me to clean up your mess, you can leave me out of it."

"If you don't want a cut in the action, fine. Arno and I are entrepreneurs. Risk takers. You can take your job and shove it."

The first warning bell chimes, signaling the imminent end of lunch.

"Are you going to park?"

Ryan shifts into overdrive. "I don't think so," he scoffs. "I have to work on my car."

"Later, champ." Arno and Kerry walk off to class.

Ryan fuels the engine in a haste to escape. And then, all at once, like the life and death moment between a pulled trigger and a falling hammer, the world dramatically slows to an incremental stop. A luscious raven-haired beauty has crossed in his path. *She's like an angel.* Ryan is transfixed as she walks in front of him. The girl looks his way and Ryan can't breathe. He swerves to miss her and continues driving, eyes locked with hers, his head turning to follow her entrancing sway.

Then, *smack!* Ryan runs into the corner of a campus security cart. Ryan hits the brakes and watches a shocked grey-haired man with a large amount of keys jangling from his waist get out of the cart and inspect the impacted area.

"Looks okay, I guess," he mumbles. "Kind of smashed right here though." The campus security looks at Ryan. "You're lucky the damage is minimal. Lunch is over, kid. You better hurry to class."

"Get out of the way! I'm not going to class." Ryan makes a shooing gesture like a prince dismissing a peasant, expecting no objections.

"Oh really? Good luck getting out of here because I already locked the gates and I'm not unlocking them again 'til seventh hour!" The man's face is reddening in anticipation for a confrontation. "Park your piecer and get to class!" The grey-haired security waits for Ryan to move on before returning to inspecting his cart for damage.

Until the school board is successful in getting rid of open campus lunch hours, Independence High still has an open campus during fourth hour for one half of the school and fifth hour for the other; however, at almost all other times while class is in session the campus is on lockdown. The only exception is before seventh hour when seniors with a short schedule are permitted to leave.

Ryan drives around the parking lot, but he is indeed gated in. *This is a goddamn teenage prison!* He parks in a space at the far end of the lot and ponders his next action. Classes have already started and he's aware of faculty who monitor the halls, sending anyone without a note to the tardy room where they are tortured with forced inaction. Sitting in a room where you aren't allowed to do anything holds zero appeal to Ryan, so he racks his brain for random things he could do instead. *This is really tops.* He takes out one of the little bottles of whiskey from his pocket and drinks it as he strategizes a plan of distraction.

12.

SAPPS IS AT HIS DESK IN THE EVERDALE POLICE Department so he can get some paperwork done. The paper shuffling is just a nuisance in his opinion. He believes his time would be better spent out in the public, protecting them from the bad guys. So instead of filling out the forms for the grave robbery case, he is attempting to complete a word search from the newspaper while absently listening to the TV. *A stage in child development. Four letters.*

"I thought America was about encouraging diversity," states a talking head from the TV that hangs from a wall mount. "Aren't you describing the opposite?"

"If you don't mind being an outcast from society, then do what you want and be an individual. It's a harder life being alone and separate from the support of the team."

"I thought you ran for City Council on an independent platform? Now you are promoting conformity?"

"I am *promoting* my book, but I believe conformity is just another word for teamwork. Isn't teamwork a good thing?"

A commotion from the front desk in the other room hits Sapps' ears. "Shut your *pie* hole, simpleton! You're obtuse!" someone is screaming.

Who is yelling out there? Sapps decides to put the paperwork on hold and go investigate.

When Sapps gets to the front desk, he sees the source of all the turmoil and shakes his head in exasperation. "Fancy!" he calls, and the middle-aged man wearing a half-shirt, dozen rings, and knee brace, turns to look Sapps up and down with disgust. Sapps notices that Fancy's eyes are bugging like he's on something. Fancy is a regular offender and well known at the Everdale Police Department for his constant yelling and tantrums as much as his varied arrest record and incessant snitching. To Sapps' way of thinking, Fancy is nothing more than a lunatic cab driver who needs to be locked up permanently. Or executed. "What's the problem here?"

The strung-out cabbie turns his full attention from verbally abusing the secretary–who is visibly relieved to no longer be the focus of Fancy's rampage–and casts a disdainful eye upon Sapps. "What's the problem? I come here to report a crime, and this obtuse bimbo, this canker sore slut, wants me to fill out a form! I'm not filling out any bureaucratic *balder*dash, see?"

"Alright Fancy, what is it you want to report? Wanda skip her fare again? I told you to stop givin' her rides."

"No, see? You have cerebral rigor mortis, Sapps? You think that walker would get away from me without paying? I'd fix her, see? That's street talk for I'd rip her eyes out and shove 'em up her open bowel! You're a cyborg, Sapps! Half machine and the rest human waste!"

Sapps tries to cut Fancy off, but Fancy just continues on his rant, getting louder, like usual, whenever he thinks someone might be trying to get a word in.

"A cyborg! A psychosomatic sycophantic synthetic slime, see? You see Sapps? Human waste!"

"What did you come here for?" Sapps yells. He's had enough.

"You want to know what I came for, huh? I'll tell you, stupid! I came to report a missing body, see?"

"You mean missin' person?"

"No, you moron! A missing body! A body, see? Corpse! Cadaver! Carcass, see? You brain-dead Dixie-do-little!"

The case! Sapps licks his lips in excitement from the good fortune. "Alright, Fancy. Why don't you come back here and I'll take your report?"

"Oh now you're happy to see me, huh, fecal juice? You want Fancy Jack Clancy to do you a favor, retard?"

"I just want to help. You came here to report a missin' person–"

"Body! Moron!"

"Body," Sapps corrects. "And I just want to help."

"I'm not filling out any goddamn forms, see? You silly sasquatch sucker!"

"Right. No forms. Just come back with me."

13

BEHIND THE COMMAND CENTER CONSOLE OF THE school office, an old woman sits occupied on the phone. She acknowledges Ryan with a quick smile as he enters. Independence High's colors are gold and white, so naturally the office is decorated in school spirit, the walls a two-tone with amber on the bottom and white above. The administration facilities are clean and organized like any other industrial building.

"Uh-huh. Right," the secretary says into the phone. "Well all of that information is in the monthly newsletter. Online."

A personified bald eagle named Libby, the school mascot, is painted from top to bottom on the far wall behind the secretary's station. Ryan wonders if the artist consciously decided to make the eagle cross-eyed or if it was just a happy accident. The fresco is signed 'Class of '98'.

"Double-u, double-u, double-u. Dot..." the secretary continues to prattle off the school's web address to the caller.

As he patiently waits his turn, Ryan takes a casual stance with his hands behind his back and let's his eyes drift across the pictures of school faculty hanging on the wall. He comes to a portrait of Mr. Jenkins, an older man with a gapped coffee-stained smile, sun red face, and wispy white hair. *What a smug looking cocksucker.*

"How may I help you?" asks the secretary. She is off the phone now and looking at Ryan expectantly, her mouth open in a motherly beam.

"Yeah...I need to fill out a claim form. For insurance."

"An insurance claim?"

"The security guy ran into my car with his golf cart and caused at *least* a thousand in damages to the...um...fender."

The woman makes a pained expression. "Ohhh, was anyone hurt?"

"No, just my car."

"Must be a nice car," she says. "Well let me see." She looks around her desk and opens up a drawer. "Harold?" she calls. "Harold!"

A guy with a belly lopping over his waist and dressed like a car salesman, partially comes out of one of the side offices. "Yes?"

"Do we have any forms? Insurance forms." She points to Ryan. "This young man had an accident in the parking lot."

"I was hit," clarifies Ryan.

The man takes in Ryan. "Do you go here?"

"I come here all the time."

The man analyzes Ryan for another second. "I have no idea," he tells the secretary before going back into his office.

The old woman returns to Ryan. "You might want to try online? We have a website now that is interactive. You can get contact information off there and email an administrator with your story." She watches him, waiting for him to accept this solution so she can add this to her list of problems solved for the day.

"I don't have the Internet."

"Well there are computers in the library."

* * *

"That's obscene."

Arno looks over his ceramics project. It was meant to be a clay recreation of one of CREASE's current pinups, but it turned out to be a pot that resembles a naked plus-size model. He responds, "It's art."

"Well I think it looks like a lumpy turd," Jill says before getting up to wet the clay for her ashtray.

"One man's treasure…" Arno glances over his shoulder at Abby, who is forming a piece at the corner table. She sees him looking and reacts by concentrating harder on pounding the air out of her clay.

"Trouble in paradise, huh?" Matt asks while etching a pattern into the pipe he made. "Are you still going together?"

Arno returns to his art. "I'm not sure about going, but we still *come* together."

Matt laughs. "That's not what I heard."

"Oh really? That's not what you heard, dipshit?" Arno adds a little more curvature to the sculpture's giant breasts. "You just watch a master." He gently picks up his still moist statue, carries it over to Abby's table, and sits next to her.

Abby continues beating the hunk of clay without making eye contact with Arno.

"Hi, Pooky," he says in a honeyed voice. "I made you something."

"I'm making you something, too."

"Yeah?" He watches her slam the clay into the table. "What is it?"

She bounces the giant chunk in her hands. "A rock."

Arno clears his throat and sees Matt laughing at him from the other table. "Don't be like that, my lil' sugar-snatch. I didn't know that was your cousin. I just got so jealous and I lost my head. Come on." He pushes the nude statue toward her. "I used the finest coils for this. It's like a piece of me," he explains. "And once it goes through the birthing in the kiln, it will be like my baby. Abby, I want you to have my baby."

Abby laughs softly and picks up the statue. "You're such a fool." She kisses him on the mouth. "But you're *my* fool."

Arno gives Matt an 'okay' sign, but Matt only flips Arno the bird.

After closer inspection of the nude female sculpture, Abby demands, "Did you put *lips* on this?"

* * *

Independence High used to have a library, but now it is called a media center. Books have been displaced or replaced by digital media and the new name is meant to reflect that change, supposedly.

Some students read at tables or lounge chairs, but otherwise the media center is not very busy. Ryan sits down at an open computer. He tries to remember his username/password and makes three attempts before finally succeeding.

He opens up the web browser, which suitably has Independence High's webpage as its home. The page layout looks very professional, apparently some school funds went into its creation. The school logo, complete with the personified eagle Libby, is in the corner of the page promoting school spirit. *This is marvelous.* Ryan opens the faculty contact page and looks through the list of administrators. *Here we go.* Ryan clicks on Mr. Jenkins and a window with a comment box pops up. Ryan types:

```
Dear Mr. Jenkins,

Why are you such a delinquent cocksucker?

Sincerely,

Eat Shit
```

Ryan hits 'send' while chuckling to himself. He looks at the clock. There's about thirty minutes left of this period. *Now to kill some more time.* Ryan opens up a search engine. He taps his head for a moment before typing in 'fun'. He looks over the results. "These sites suck."

Ryan searches for 'hot pussy'. He clicks on a Leila site that seems promising, but a page reading 'FORBIDDEN' shows up. Ryan shakes his head in disappointment.

"What are you looking for?" Arno asks in a hushed voice appropriate for the media center. He takes a seat at a terminal next to Ryan. "I thought you were going to work on your car?"

Ryan doesn't seem to be perceptive of Arno's low-key manner as he vocalizes normally, "I'm just wasting time. I got stuck here."

"That sucks," Arno empathizes.

"What are you doing? You have a class in the media center?"

"I'm out on a bathroom pass." Arno peeks around the media room as if someone might be listening. He notices a brunette girl reading a book entitled *Rust, Wheat, and Beige: The American Reality* giving him and Ryan a dirty look. Arno makes a kissy face at her and she rolls her eyes. "I needed a break from ceramics. It was getting hot in there."

"I'm so bored." Ryan sounds extra loud in the subdued atmosphere. "School is shit."

"The Internet is a great place to kill time." Arno has logged on and is accessing his email. "That's about all it does. Have you ever tried searching for yourself? Sometimes I do that when I want to waste some time. I'm on like six sites including my profile page. Or you can always piss people off in a forum. You can't really get any porn off these school computers since they blocked all the good sites."

"I noticed." Ryan types his name into the search bar, but elicits zero items. Arno catches the results.

"You don't even show up once," Arno snickers with a look over his shoulder, and drops his voice back to library level. "That's pretty weak."

"I guess I don't exist."

Arno signs off. "I have to get back before the hour's out. I'll see you later." He leaves with a pat on Ryan's head and a suspicious eyeing of the media center.

Ryan gets an idea. He types "Jeffrey Neil" into the search engine. This time he gets over a dozen results. He sits up in his chair and clicks on one of the links. A page opens up that contains an article about a marathon involving forty-one year old Jeffrey Neil from New Fillmore. After a moment studying the accompanied photo, Ryan decides that this is not the same Jeffrey Neil he is searching for.

The school bell chimes and the period is over.

Ryan clicks on the next search result.

"What have we here?" He has come across the obituary for Jeffrey Neil and reads it aloud to himself. "Jeffrey C. Neil died February sixth. He was only eighteen. He is survived by his mother. Memorial will be held on February tenth at three at Liberty Funeral Home." Ryan stares at the page for a moment. "This doesn't tell me diddly-do."

A new class has entered the media center for study period and the bell chimes again to signal the end of pass period. Ryan clicks on the following result in the search engine and a window entitled 'Jeffrey's Online Journal' starts downloading. This site looks very basic and doesn't appear to have many graphics. Ryan reads from the journal:

```
December 19, 1998
A Real American. Maybe I'm the only true one
left?


December 14, 1998
It's good to have a sense of humor about the
past. You can't change it. But it is good to be
serious about the present, so less laughter is
needed to overcome pain in the future.


December 13, 1998
I get off work and go to the swinger's club
```

"Excuse me," interjects a pigeon-faced lady, "would you mind getting off the computer? These are reserved for my class."

Ryan glances from her to the kid wearing a sports coat behind her who needs to use the computer. "Okay," says Ryan. "Let me just print this out."

"Hurry up," the teacher says coldly.

Ryan sends the print job of the online journal to the communal printer and relinquishes the seat.

"Have you already set up an account, Soji?" the lady is asking the kid in the sportcoat as Ryan goes to the print station.

As if fate existed, standing alone at the printer, is the same seductive raven-haired girl Ryan fell in love with an hour ago in the parking lot. She is busy collecting pages from the printer and stacking them on the table next to it.

Ryan smiles at his fortune, but at the same time is overcome with nervous anxiety. His heart lodges in his throat and his hands start to quiver. With a deep breath, he gathers his courage and approaches the angelic beauty. "Hi," he pops out.

The raven-haired girl barely reacts.

Ryan's ego and desire force him to continue. "Do you remember me?" he asks.

She gives him a fleeting glimpse, then shakes her head. "Am I supposed to?"

Ryan can't believe what he is hearing. "I saw you earlier today. In the parking lot."

"Who are you?" she asks absently as she continues stacking the papers steadily streaming from the printer.

"I'm Ryan."

She suddenly seems interested in the conversation. "You go to school here?"

Ryan tries to play it cool and props himself on the printer. "Sometimes."

"Are you coming to the social tomorrow?"

"Do you, do you want to go?" Ryan stutters.

"Yeah, I'll be there." She hands him one of the papers she has collected from the printer–a flyer for the school social. "I'm promoting it. You should come."

"Alright." Ryan folds the flyer and puts it in his pocket. "What's your name?"

"Mallory. I'm sorry, what's yours again?"

He replies with irritation, "It's *Ryan*."

"Okay." Mallory's print job has finished. "See you later."

Ryan watches Mallory walk away as he waits for his pages to come out of the printer, completely thrown off by her lack of interest. *Is she playing games? How could she not recognize me?*

He could have sworn that the electric moment they shared in the parking lot was mutual. *She doesn't want me to go to the social; she is just promoting it.* Ryan's pages start coming out of the printer. *But she smells so delicious. Like blueberry muffins.*

14

A MODERN MASTERPIECE OF PERSONAL LUXURY AND performance descends upon the dirt parking area for Jalisco's Mini-Mart like a man-eating shark in the kiddy pool. This sleek mechanized beast, a 1967 Buick Riviera, is deep red, almost black, lovingly customized with added chrome trim to enhance the original aesthetics of the model. About a dozen decals decorate its left side like fighter plane kills and the license plate reads, 'R I P'.

Out of the nightmarish auto steps a tall man, his left ear looks like it has been gnawed off and the skin over his gaunt face and hairless scalp is stretched so tightly it gives him the appearance of a skeleton. He gives Jalisco's a cool once-over from behind dark sunglasses before entering.

Inside, a soon-to-be fossil of a man stands behind the checkout counter helping a customer. The customer drums his fingers on the counter, agitated by the pace of the old clerk who is adding the items together on a piece of paper. The clerk's penmanship suffers from a severe case of old man shivers.

"Look Jalisco," says the customer with little patience, "I have one bag of chips, that's one fifty, a O Henry, fifty cents, two sodas, seventy-five cents each, and a bottle of tangerine dream, for two seventy-five." The old man isn't listening and continues to tally the items onto paper.

The man in black strolls over to the beer cooler to peruse the tall cans.

"Alright so that's...uh," the impatient customer does some calculations, "two and one fifty...*five*, six, six twenty-five. Simple."

The man with the mangled left ear snatches one of the cans, rolls it over in his sinewy left hand, and rubs his thumb over the pink price tag. He takes the beer and stands in line at the checkout.

"Okay?" the customer is asking.

The old man finishes his calculations. "Six twenty-five," he gasps.

The customer pulls out some cash. "Here you go. Six twenty-five," the customer says, laying down the money. The old man picks it up and starts counting. "It's all there. I'll see you later, Mister Jalisco." The customer takes the purchases and scurries away.

Mr. Jalisco opens the register and divvies the cash into it while the skeletal man watches coolly. Mr. Jalisco closes the register, slowly turns his attention to the man in opaque sunglasses and the beer he is holding, and asks tiredly, "Anything else?"

The man stretches a bony forefinger and points at the tall can in his grasp. "Do you remember selling any of these yesterday?" he asks Mr. Jalisco in a voice like grinding gears.

"Yesterday?" Mr. Jalisco tries to understand the question.

A woman who has not been treated kindly by time, with bad teeth and frizzy hair, ambles into the liquor mart with a hand on her hip and goes up to the counter. "What's happenin' missa Jalisco?" she greets. "I'll take one o' them pig knuckles when ya got a chance."

"Pig...knuckle?" Mr. Jalisco turns around to get the stool he needs to reach the jar on the high shelf behind the register.

"Wait a sec..." The skeletal man twitches in annoyance by the interjection, but clamps his mouth shut and grinds his teeth.

An aluminum can crunches under the stool as Mr. Jalisco laboriously moves it into place under the large jar of pork knuckles. The sound attracts the attention of the man in black.

The grim man swoops behind the counter to catch the attention of the old store owner and indicates toward the can under the stool. "He was just here, wasn't he?"

Mr. Jalisco has rolled up his sleeve and is reaching his hand into the jar of pork knuckles. He is torn between trying to comprehend what he is being asked and obtaining the correct item the woman is directing him toward.

"Just ya keep still now," the dirty woman says to the man with the mangled ear. "Missa Jalisco will get ta ya." She returns to Mr. Jalisco. "No not that one. The big one. The *big* one! Yeah, that one right there."

Mr. Jalisco steps off the stool–his arm dripping in pig juice–and gives the woman her knuckle.

The man of mystery snatches the can from under the stool and holds it up in front of the old clerk's nose. "Who drank this beer?" he growls between gritted teeth.

"Woah guy, ya needs ta calm yaself," the filthy woman says excitedly. "There's more in the coola."

Mr. Jalisco's jitters intensify from the commotion and his jaw works silently.

The ominous man in black swings the can from Mr. Jalisco's face to the trampy woman. His speech remains level, though his body-language screams like a fire alarm. "I am looking for the person who comes here and buys this type of beer. It may be the same person that drank from this very same can. What do you know?"

"I don' know nothin'. And he don' know nothin' neither," cries the woman.

The ghostly man slowly lifts his sinewy left hand, the black sleeve falling to reveal the red, orange, and violet intertwining in jagged art down from his wrist toward his elbow, and extends his index finger. Mr. Jalisco stares at the jagged finger as if it held a great secret. Then the skeletal man purposefully, and very lightly, touches the tip of the outstretched digit to the forehead of Mr. Jalisco. Just for a moment and then his hand is back at his side. The driver of the abyss-red Riviera pitches the tall can into the trash on his way out of the store.

"You okay, missa Jalisco?" the vagrant woman asks in worry.

Mr. Jalisco is clutching his chest, but nods that he is okay.

15

RYAN SHUFFLES INTO HIS DISASTROUS ROOM, THE TV still blinking on the dresser and murmuring quietly. He takes a few test sniffs, but he can't tell if the dead body propped up in the corner has added any noticeable stench to the normal funk.

"How was your day?" he asks the corpse.

The corpse continues to rot peacefully.

Ryan turns the ceiling fan on low, the light off, and after struggling to remove his shirt, throws it on the ground with his other temporarily discarded clothes.

The sun's golden rays peek between the bedroom window and the blinds, casting a warm magical glow into the room.

"I read your obituary. On the Internet," Ryan says, sprawling out on his bed and working the aches from his muscles. "I wonder if your mom's still alive. She probably misses you, huh?" Ryan yawns widely. "You sure don't say much." He laughs softly in his weariness. "You stupid corpse."

* * *

Ryan stands outside of a cozy suburban home, reading a sign on the door that says 'Celebrate Each Day'. The home's red door contrasts with the blue exterior walls and trim, but Ryan feels only warmth from the house. He can sense it, like it radiates benevolence. An elderly woman wearing a muumuu answers Ryan's knock.

"Hi." Ryan clears his throat. "Mrs. Neil?"

"Yes?" The woman tilts her head back to peer at Ryan through her bifocals.

"I was wondering if I could talk to you for a minute."

"Hold on," she says before shutting the door on him.

He taps his foot, staring at the sign on the door. A shadow darkens the peephole from inside the house. He knocks again. A second harder knock, and she cracks the door open. "It's about your son," he quickly speaks.

"My son?" She gives Ryan a curious look. "Jeffrey?"

Ryan nods. "It will just be a moment."

"Well...alright." Mrs. Neil smiles. "Come on in." She welcomes Ryan into her bright, pleasant home. The inside is painted a sky blue, the trim along the walls is an apple red. On closer look, Ryan realizes the red trim is patterned with birds of some sort, and the ceiling is decorated to look like clouds. As he follows her to the living room, the feeling of goodness he sensed outside the home grows larger.

Even the air seems to sparkle.

Mrs. Neil sits in her recliner next to a table with a gigantic ornate lamp that looks like a bird's talon and motions Ryan to sit on the suede sofa.

"You were friends with Jeff?" she asks.

"Yes ma'am." Ryan tries to get comfortable on the sofa. The natural tan suede looks snuggly soft, but it seems made of granite, and the lamp next to Mrs. Neil is making Ryan sweat. He can see light swirl from the top and bottom of the shade, twinkling blue and red.

The swirling, almost tangible light, dances around the room. The lamp seems to be the source of the feeling of goodness that permeates the Neil residence.

Mrs. Neil looks Ryan over. "Hmm, that's unusual," she says, shifting in her seat. "You'd been what? Six when he passed?"

"I don't know. Nine?"

Mrs. Neil doesn't seem to acknowledge the solid light that shimmers around her. "What did you say your name was?"

"Alphonzo."

Mrs. Neil's eyes go distant on the TV while she searches her memory. A fish-lipped evangelist wearing a purple wig is on the television, hugging starving children of other countries. "I don't remember him mentioning you." She dismisses this with a smile. "But Jeff was a popular boy. Everyone loved him. Everyone. I miss him so much."

"He was a charmer," agrees Ryan. He squints through the rays at the silhouette of Mrs. Neil. The light around her glows too brightly now for Ryan to see into.

"He was my pride and joy," she whispers dreamily.

"That's beautiful, Mrs. Neil." Ryan watches the light that has emanated from the ornate lamp begin to congregate at a spot in the middle of the room.

Mrs. Neil is glassy-eyed as she daydreams about her dearly departed son. "What is it you wanted to talk about, Alphonzo?"

"What if I told you that you could see your son again?"

The light at the center of the room is congealing into a form, almost recognizable.

"What do you mean?" she asks carefully.

Someone raps at the door.

"Who the fuck is it *now*?" Mrs. Neil belts in annoyance. But before she can get out of her seat, the door flies open.

Standing in the doorway, almost as if it were held up by an unseen cable from heaven, is the festering corpse of Mrs. Neil's son.

Her eyes open almost as wide as her mouth. "My boy!" she exclaims. "You've come home."

The old woman rushes to wrap her arms around the corpse of her far-dead child. The long awaited homecoming has come at last. Tears of joy flood down her cheeks. A moment she has only dreamed of. The dream of the loved returning home and the nightmare of reality dismissed as fictitious. This is the moment Mrs. Neil thought she would never see until the time when she herself was called back.

Ryan is warmed by the raw emotion of the moment, his chest aches with the beauty of the mother and son reunion and his head strains from holding back tears. Mrs. Neil laughs jubilantly as the tears stream down her face, and kisses the greenish face of the corpse in her rapture.

The jaw of the corpse drops open and the reddish-blue radiant light that has solidified into something almost humanoid, appears to be sucked or vacuumed into the dark maw of decay, and absorbed in a flash.

Ryan wakes with the deep emotion still bright in his mind. He sits up, wipes a damp eye and scrutinizes Jeffrey, who sits in the corner of the room. He takes a trembling breath. The sun no longer peeks through the blinds of his bedroom window.

"Let's go for a ride, dude."

16

MOST OF THE TRAFFIC LIGHTS ARE BLINKING YELLOW, due to the late hour, as Ryan cruises through the standard streets of Everdale in his 1980 brown Chrysler, destinationless, with Jeffrey for a navigator.

"It's good to go driving sometimes," Ryan tells Jeffrey insightfully. "It can really clear my head." Ryan studies the town as he drives. A stoplight, a brick wall, a stucco building, a parking lot, and a strip mall. A strip mall, a stoplight, a stucco building, a parking lot, and Ryan becomes irritated by the insipidness.

"This place is so bland ...so blah!" Ryan addresses Jeffrey. "I got to get out of this trap, you know? Before I end up like you. Just a matter of time, right?" Ryan hops the curb as he pulls The Defiler into Super Tacos UnLTD. "I'm gonna get a burrito, yo. Then let's go to the park and chill, alright?"

The city recreation area glows a burnt orange from dim safety lights, where Ryan sits at the bottom of a short slide, and Jeffrey lies in the tire swing.

A dog barks a little ways away in the melancholy midnight. Ryan washes down his burrito with the beer he retrieved from his glove box–it's warm but still thirst-quenching–and an amused grin lights up his face as he continues from where he left off in the printout of Jeffrey's online journal.

```
December 13, 1998
I get off work and go to the swinger's club
with Adler. We get discounted, but the place
sucks. Meet some strippers from the club. Holly
invites me to breakfast. I have this thing on
my nose. We eat at a greasy spoon me her Adler
guy & girlfriend stripper. Adler gets repulsed
by stripper talk I express my fears of getting
fired. We leave them and walk next door for a
beer wait at bus stop because the Trans is
still down hippie asks for 1.50 to ride bus I
say bus is only $1 here isn't it he replies he
was hoping to get some breakfast Adler says
breakfast isn't 50¢ bro. I go to work at 6:00
hm? To many people scheduled to work.
```

```
December 10, 1998
Death is freedom. Life goes on.
```

```
December 2, 1998
In a free world, the good people will rise
to the top, and the bad will sink. Bringing
everyone to the middle is the only way to
attempt to make people equal. Making people
equal can only be done by limiting freedom.
```

```
How do people become equal? Limit choices.
Limiting choices limits freedom of choice.
Limiting freedom of choice limits freedom.
How do you limit freedom? Expand the government.
Who runs the government? Vultures.
Who benefits from equality? Vultures and Turkeys.
```

"What do birds have to do with equality and freedom?" Ryan complains. "Were you a chicken-bugger, Jeffrey? I bet you were, you sick bastard," Ryan laughs and takes another sip from his beer.

November 22, 1998
Is anyone out there? I put shit on the world
wide web and I feel more alone than ever. Go
fuck yourself.

November 21, 1998
Adler says that we'll be out of here in a few
weeks. It seems like I'll never get free of
here, but he tells me he's got it handled

November 16, 1998
Life is easier when you have minimal choices. An
illusion of choice. An assortment of basically
the same choice. An illusion of freedom. The
important decisions have less options.

Vultures promote equality and political
correctness because they want more power.
Equality limits choice. Limiting choice
restricts freedom. The less freedom, the more
power the vultures have.

Ryan squints his eyes from the headache he's getting due to
reading in the low light. He stretches his legs and says to Jeffrey,
"You're kind of ridiculous," before reading on; refreshed and ready
to dive back into Jeffrey's meanderings.

November 10, 1998
We Are All Destroyed Equal

November 9, 1998
Christian bitch came over today and after she
was talking about me being a Gemini, having
jesus shit, why I don't believe in God or
Astrology, about why she is not having sex
before marriage. Every time I tried to talk with
her she would laugh at me, interrupt and/or make
a grand judgement about me. I told her that if
she wanted respect (for ridiculous beliefs) then
she should show respect to other people. She
said she was leaving because now she saw that I
wasn't as down to earth as her. ?????

November 3, 1998
Why must there be so many detailed tampon
commercials on TV?

October 23, 1998
Besides turkeys and eagles there is

Ryan's reading is interrupted by a beam of white light flooding on his Chrysler from a police cruiser. *Shit!* Ryan sets his beer in the sand, and goes to meet the patrol. The policeman has gotten out of the car and is inspecting the interior of the old Newport with his flashlight. The officer is alerted to Ryan approaching and shines the light in his eyes.

"This your clunker, son?" asks the officer.

"It's my car," says Ryan.

"Whatcha doin' out here?"

"Just hanging out."

The Adonis-looking officer nears Ryan and looks him over with the light. He shines the beam toward the park and over to the tire swing, but probably can't really identify Jeffrey from that far. Ryan reads the officer's nametag: REEVES.

"You kids out here doin' drugs?" Reeves interrogates.

"Nope." Ryan waves Jeffrey's journal in the air. "Just studying."

"Don't bullshit me, son." Officer Reeves just looks at Ryan for a moment, then points the light to the ground. "Park's closed. You can't be out here this late."

"Really? I didn't know a park could be closed."

"Well it is," Reeves grunts.

"Alright."

"You have to leave."

"We will."

Reeves flashes the light back in Ryan's eyes. "Don't let me catch you out here again." He turns off his flashlight with a sigh. "Pass that on to your buddy."

Ryan watches Reeves get in the patrol car and coast away. "Damn this town is weak." He goes back and collects his beer and Jeffrey. He decides to not take any more chances this evening and puts Jeffrey in the trunk for the ride home. Some people in Everdale might be prejudiced of citizens in Jeffrey's condition and less than understanding of those who associate with his kind.

17

THE MAN DRESSED IN BEREAVEMENT BLACK KNUCKLES his mangled left ear while staring at the unfinished 289 onramp leading out of Everdale. He tilts his head to see hundreds of feet in the air to the blockaded freeway's precipitous ending. With a grunt, he spits out of the dark Riviera's window before turning the car away from the onramp, down into the depths of mundane suburban opulence.

A sudden turbulence rattles the Buick as an old brown sedan breezes precariously close. Watching the speeding car screech to a jerky stop at a red light, the gaunt man grips the steering wheel and shakes his bald head in disgust. He gently eases his Riviera to the stoplight and peers at the reckless driver of the racing junk pile.

The driver of the other car goes slack-jawed at sight of the visually impressive Buick. The young man, with eyes filled in a mix of envy, dreaminess, and appreciation, salutes the Buick with a beer and then guzzles from its contents.

The light turns green, but before the young driver takes off, the man in the devil-red Buick notices the pink tag on the can.

A fury crosses over the man's lank face. He slams the Riviera's gas like stomping on a tin can, and tears after the brown car already a little distance ahead. He easily catches up to the sedan and zooms alongside, motioning and commanding the young driver to stop.

The grim man sounds the Riviera's horn, he lays on it, but the other driver looks over and only urges the sedan faster, whooping, as if this were an impromptu street race. The young driver, probably miffed that the Buick will not be outrun, throws his beer can out the window and it clatters across the windshield.

The skeletal man's eyebrows furrow in a detonation of anger and he whips under his seat to pull out a Colt Double Eagle semi-automatic pistol.

The young man catches sight of the weapon, flinches, and veers sharply, careening over a median and onto a side street, sending a 'Speed In Everdale, Go Directly To Jail' sign flying. The Buick is effectively cut off so the man spins around to correct, but the brown car is nowhere in sight. In a dire rage, the skeletal man fumes from behind the opaque glasses, clenching the pistol in his red orange hand.

18

"SO IF YOU COULD COME BACK, SAY FOR A DAY, WHAT would you do? I mean, is there anything you regret doing?"

"Dying."

"Come on now! Really. What are you into?"

"Are you blind, dude? I'm dead. I don't care about anything."

"Nothing?"

"What do *you* care about, Ryan?"

"I don't know. Getting out of here. I care about that. And girls."

"And digging up dead people."

"Hey, it wasn't my idea to dig you up."

"But you went along with it. You're an accomplice."

"What's eating you? I would've thought you'd be thanking me. Didn't you have fun, too?"

"Maybe."

"That's it? Is that all the end's like?"

"...dark."

* * *

Ryan stops for his usual afternoon pick-me-up. A guy in a uniform is outside Jalisco's Mini-Mart replacing the sign with one that reads 'Super Convenience UnLTD'. The normal mishmash of advertisements that hung in Jalisco's windows have been removed and replaced with newer ads in a more organized concept. The place seems cleaner, sterile, as if it was following a well-scripted formula.

"What's going on here?" Ryan asks himself.

When Ryan walks into the store, he learns that Jalisco's has changed on the inside as well. For one, Old Man Jalisco is no longer behind the counter. Instead, a thirty-something greaseball wearing a polo shirt tucked into khakis stands behind the register.

"Hello," the new clerk says robotically, without even glancing at Ryan. There aren't any other customers around, not even Wanda.

The ranchero music that Jalisco used to play from a tiny stereo has been replaced by the dull hum of Leila's current single emanating from new ceiling speakers.

The eerie transformation of his habitual breakfast stop heaves Ryan's brain into a discombobulated crisis. Glazed, he grabs his usual couple tall cans and brings them to the checkout.

"Will this be all?" drones the clerk.

"Where's Mr. Jalisco?" Ryan asks, spilling his collected change all over the counter.

"He died."

Ryan is shocked by the news. "That really *sucks*." He purses his lips in sadness and takes a stilling breath. "Can you hand me that CREASE right there?"

"May I see your ID please, sir?"

"Huh? Oh yeah." Ryan hands over Alphonzo Casañas's ID, which the clerk inspects.

"Um, this isn't you."

"What? Let me see that." Ryan snatches the ID from the clerk and inspects it for himself. "Yeah, that's me. Alphonzo. I just got different hair now."

"Get out of here kid," laughs the clerk. "I can't sell to you."

"What are you talking about? I buy here all the time!"

"Sorry. Policy." The clerk points to a cardboard sign next to the register that reads 'Under 21? No Fun! Zip-Nada-None'. "Nice try though."

"Screw this place!" Ryan yells, collecting his coins. "Give me my money that fell back there!"

"Here's a dollar," the clerk says, pulling a bill from the register. "Get the hell out of here."

Ryan snags the money and heads out of the store. "This treatment is revolting!"

FOR THE BIRDS

19

RYAN SITS IN HIS CAR, THINKING OF HIS NEXT MOVE
and studying the dollar the clerk gave him. *Novus Ordo Seclorum.*
I am broke. He folds the bill and slips it into his pocket with a
heavy sigh. *This is going to be a rubbish day.* Stupified, Ryan starts
his car and in a few incoherent moments, he finds himself parked
at Independence High.

It's fourth hour lunch, but the campus seems relatively quiet.
Ryan–practically in a sleepwalking state–makes his way into the
cafetorium, a large room used for serving lunches that also functions
as an assembly area when needed. Because it is lunchtime for
half the school, the cafetorium is currently bustling with activity;
however, it's all distant to Ryan. Over the platform on the far side of
the room, a large handcrafted banner advertises tonight's social with
big malformed glittery letters. *I'll kill some time here until someone
gets out of class. Maybe Arno or Kerry can hook up the beer.*

Ryan sits at a table and finds where he left off in Jeffrey's
journal, and even though some parts he had previously read might
be to blame for his migraine, his nagging morbid curiosity prods
him to learn more about his new friend.

83

October 23, 1998
Besides turkeys and eagles there is a third type
of human: vultures. Vultures are people that are
unable to exist without feeding from eagles or
turkeys. Vultures are any person or entity that
relies on the fruits of other's labors. Vultures
are the originators of false mantras like
equality. They lack integrity.

A vulture is not a bird of prey, but of death.
Its only base of survival is its cunning
instinct to feed on death. But the man with a
vulture's heart is much worse. This man promotes
the death of free spirit. This man with a
vulture's heart feeds on the carcasses of eagles
and turkeys with dead spirits.

Politicians are vultures. Moneylenders are
vultures. Religious leaders are vultures.
Lawyers are vultures.

October 4, 1998
Adler introduced me to his connection. The guy
is an asswipe but he says Jack told him if we
play our cards right we can be real players. I
don't trust him. Adler says I'm being a wussy.
Get oil change.

October 2, 1998
Here's a tune I wrote:

```
+-9------------+---9--7----5--+------------------+--------------+ ------
+--------------+--------------+----------9--+--------7---+-5------4---+--2---
+-7------------+---7--5----3--+------------------+----------------+-------
+--------------+--------------+----------7---+--------5---+-3------2---+--0---
```

September 25, 1998
'Eagle' or 'turkey' is a measurement of a
man's heart: courage, strength of character,
independent spirit, pursuit of greatness, and
perception of reality.

Ryan scans down and sees the next journal entry. He leans back
and stretches his torso while his eyes wander over the cafetorium
of students he doesn't recognize. He takes a deep breath and tries
to soak in what he just read. His stomach growls loudly, and he
wonders what he'll eat for lunch. He folds the journal and puts it in
his pocket on his way over to the meal court.

The lunches in Independence High's cafetorium are provided by the usual UnLTD restaurants–Quickie Food, Super Tacos, and Original Oriental–and the cafetorium resembles a mall or airport food court.

Ryan's mouth waters as he gets in line and looks over the menus. He pulls out his dollar, then looks back over the items.

"Welcome to the Independence Cafetorium, what can I get you?" the old woman at the counter asks Ryan.

"Yeah, uh, I'd like one taquito."

"One order of taquitos. Is that it?"

"No, just *one* taquito," he says, holding up his index finger. "I don't have enough for a whole order."

"We accept credit or Libby Dollars?"

"I don't have any *credit*," Ryan says through clenched teeth.

"Well, I can give you one taquito," she says, "but I would still have to charge for an order. I don't have a button for *one* taquito"

Ryan sees that this conversation is going nowhere. He is about to leave the cafetorium when his stomach reminds him of his hunger. He anxiously looks around and spots a vending machine. He goes over and checks out its contents. *I want that roast beef! Damn, it's too much. I'll just get some jerky.* Ryan inserts the dollar, but when he presses the buttons, nothing happens.

"That machine is out of order," says a geeky kid sitting nearby.

"Why didn't you tell me before?" Ryan asks hotly.

The geek takes a bite from his Foodables™ and shrugs. "You have to call the vendor's eight-hundred number and they'll send you a check."

Ryan is infuriated. He snags the Foodables™ from the geek's clutches and devours the contents as the geek stares at him, eyes full of pained turmoil. "Thanks for your help, pud." He tosses the empty Foodables™ container in the face of the geek and checks the clock. *Kerry and Arno will be out of class soon.*

He goes back to his seat in the cafetorium and pulls out the online journal. With determination, he decides to tackle some more of Jeffrey's pre-mortem thoughts.

```
September 24, 1998
A ton of feathers is equal to a ton of hammers,
but they are not the same. How many feathers
does it take to equal the same weight as 1
hammer? Thousands? Can turkeys even be measured
on the same scale as an eagle? Can they even
compare? When baking a cake, does a cup of flour
equal a cup of sand? Not if you want a well made
cake. Thus I say to you that it does indeed
matter what ingredient is used and that a cup of
sand is not equal to a cup of flour because flour
is not the same as sand.
```

Ryan blinks to clear his eyes and dedicates himself to learning about his new companion before continuing on, promising himself to read faster, to let the words wash over him, to soak in the flood of Jeffrey's written thoughts.

```
I tell you that a soul can be measured the same
way as flour and sand, as feathers and hammers,
as turkeys and eagles. 'We are all the same'
isn't true; therefore, 'we are all equal' isn't
true.
```

```
So how do we know if we are a turkey or an
eagle? It is difficult. For someone that is a
turkey at heart, this feat is futile, as you
will forever live as a turkey with the sight
and perception of a turkey. Only eagles have a
higher perception. Only eagles can uncloud their
senses from false mantras and see the world.
```

```
September 24, 1998
Free hearts are eagles. A turkey that is told it
is an eagle, may believe so, but it doesn't make
it true. The real tragedy is when an eagle is
made to believe it is a turkey. This is what our
society has done under the mantra of equality.
Since equality has been confused with sameness.
Of course people see equality in the terms of
sameness. X does not equal Y because X is not
the same as Y.
```

The lunch bell rings for fifth hour and Ryan tries to finish the last bit of the entry quickly before the cafetorium is overrun with new hungry students. A couple nerds have already burst through the doors, racing each other to the meal line.

```
Why must an eagle be made to walk because
a turkey can't fly? Who does the pursuit of
equality benefit if not the least noble of
beasts?
```

Ryan folds the journal back into his pocket and exits the cafetorium. Rollo and Doyle are walking together to the media center and he thinks he sees Mallory driven off campus in a GTO. He spots Arno entertaining several other kids with a very animated storytelling. Denise and Kerry sit near him, making out with each other. Ryan continues to the parking lot without greeting them.

"All these people are turkeys." Ryan realizes.

20

NUMBNESS HAS FALLEN OVER RYAN. IN HIS ROOM, the TV still flickers, clothes are still strewn over his floor and bed, and a human corpse by the name of Jeffrey still sits in his seat. Ryan stares out the window, watching two birds peck at each other. Clouds block the sun, making the view from Ryan's room dull and grey, with the amount of luster contained in a box of manure. *How am I going to get out of here? I have no money. Jobs I can get here will just pull me in further. Everdale is like a black hole. A giant mass of empty gravitational pull, sucking in the souls around it. I feel Everdale sucking me in, trying to keep me here. It gets bigger, and stronger. Am I strong enough to escape?*

"Am I an eagle, Jeffrey?" Ryan wonders. He gazes at his motionless friend in the corner of his room. A beetle crawls out of Jeffrey's mouth. "Will I only be free when I die?"

"Death is the poor man's freedom, and the rich man's judgment."

"So I have to be rich to live free?"

"As long as you live in the prison of society."

"That's how the cookie crumbles, huh?"

"What are you doing here?"

"I ain't doin' shit. There's nothing to do."

"You got to get out there. While you can."

"And do what?"

"I don't know, but that's where the world is. One day you'll be like me, and you won't have to worry about it anymore. On that day, you'll wish you had this time back."

"Everyone out there is a damn turkey. I can't relate to these people!"

"You want to be an eagle? You got to go for it, dude. There is no waiting for tomorrow. Your problem is you have it too easy. You sit around all day. There is a fruit of life that can only be tasted after struggle. You have to fight. Conquer life. Be fearless. Be an eagle."

Ryan's heart races with a somber desire and understanding. The clouds move past, unveiling the sun's golden rays to drench the world outside Ryan's bedroom in brilliant light, revealing the Earth's vibrancy in all its fantastic shimmering colors.

21

RYAN PULLS UP TO SUPER CONVENIENCE UNLTD AND leaves The Defiler running. "Watch the car," he tells Jeffrey, who matches Ryan's disguise of sunglasses and hat.

He runs into the store with his heart thumping hollow incentives in his chest. The clerk is busy helping a customer, and there are a couple other people in the store, but Ryan acknowledges no one and goes directly to the beer cooler.

Taking a deep breath to brace himself, he grabs a twenty-four case and just walks out of the store and into his car without looking back. "Let's move!" he says to his co-conspirator.

Jeffrey stays in stealth mode as Ryan casually drives away from the crime scene, glancing in the rearview. No one is chasing them.

"Success, Jeffrey!" He howls in celebration at the mission accomplished. This was just step one. Gathering fuel.

Back in his room, Ryan is a few beers down in the case, already making a dent in organizing his room. He already feels better. His surroundings are less cluttered, and now, so is his mind.

The TV is muttering along as he finishes putting the last of his clothes away. A sudden rage passes through him, triggered by the voices and images that he realizes are poisoning his brain. Hypnotic messages urging him to relax. Programming for the masses. He removes the tire-iron he stores between his mattresses, and with a triumphant yell, he smashes the television to smithereens.

Ryan cries out in jubilation from how invigorated he feels. The trash is removed from his room, including a lot of the knick-knacks. He has only left one poster on the wall, one of Arnold Schwarzenegger describing the meaning of life.

"I'm done organizing," Ryan says to Jeffrey, who is lying in his bed. Step two complete. "Looks like it's time to get ready."

Ryan is in his open garage, now empty of all the old boxes, doing some seated bicep curls next to his workbench. He's enjoying the shades of pink, red, purple, and blue in the sky of the setting sun and the fresh air of being outside. He does a set of pushups then checks his pump in the bar mirror hanging in the garage. *We'll see what tonight has to offer. An eagle has to leave its nest to hunt.*

22

THE PARKING LOT IS PACKED FOR THE BIG SOCIAL
at Independence High. The entire school–maybe two schools–must
be in attendance. Ryan bypasses searching for a spot in the lot and
drives up onto the walkway near the entrance and parks The Defiler.
He is wearing his sexiest duds for the occasion, but has decided
to keep the fingerless gloves for style. The muffled thump of the
dance music can be heard from the outside of the closed cafetorium
doors. Ryan surveys the scene with a deep breath and checks his
appearance one more time in the vanity mirror before he gets out
of the vehicle. At the door, a couple of teens act as sentries for the
event: Rollo and Doyle.

Doyle, in his oversized suit jacket and his greased back bowl-
cut hair, sneers as Ryan approaches. "You got a ticket, Ace?"

"Ticket? No, I got invited." Ryan tries to pull it off, but he wasn't
expecting these two stooges to be working the door.

"Invited?" Rollo snorts. He sits at a folding table with a cashbox
in front of him. "Tickets are ten bucks, Ryan. You cheap prick."

"Come on guys. Be cool."

The two brothers look at each other, but Rollo shakes his head. "You got to pay to play, bud. Everyone needs a ticket."

Ryan makes like he's looking for his wallet. "Hold on. I guess I forgot my stuff in my car. Just a second."

"Sure."

Ryan walks back to his car and pretends to be unlocking it while watching the two doormen. They are busy acting their part, charging a couple students admission. He makes a crouching run around the corner of the cafetorium in an espionage-inspired moment and presses his back against the wall. He waits for a second to listen, but all he hears is his own heavy breathing, no signs of pursuit. He continues around the back of the cafetorium building looking for a way in.

Ryan tries the gym room doors. Locked. Something in the air catches his attention. A musky odor. He takes a few test sniffs into the night. *Someone's smoking.* Ryan follows his nose further around the back of the school to three students huddling in the shadows of the theater building entrance. The smokers hear him approaching and they try to hide the joint.

"Who is that?" one of them demands.

Ryan puts on his friendly face. "What's happening guys?"

"Ryan?" says a familiar voice. "Yo guys, it's only Ryan,"

Ryan is now close enough to make out Arno and two others, Abby and a fat guy Charles. "Huzzah!" he salutes with a wide grin. "Is that door open?"

"We have it propped open," Abby says, pointing to a wood block keeping the door ajar.

"Do you have a ticket?" Charles asks. "I'm supposed to be watching this entrance."

"Hell no," Ryan says proudly.

"Don't be a burg, Chuck," Arno says, toking from the herb. He then holds it up for Abby.

Ryan holds his fingers out. "You seen Mallory in there?"

Arno hands over the spliff to Ryan and asks, "Who?"

"She's got dark hair, cute as hell," Ryan describes.

"I know who you're talking about," says Charles. "We're in student council together. I got a class with her too. She's incredible sexy. Way too good for someone with your credit score."

"She here?" Ryan asks after puffing from the tightly packed and rapidly shrinking stub.

"Haven't seen her," Charles says, taking the jay out of Ryan's fingers and finishing it off. Charles holds the smoke in his lungs for a bit before exhaling with a light cough.

"Let's go back in," Abby suggests.

Ryan follows her and Arno through the doors of the theater building and into a passage for restrooms, while Charles stays behind to continue his duty as security. The pumping dance music grows louder with every foot forward until they step through large drapes and Ryan is hit with a wall of throbbing sound. The theater building has been transformed into a dance club with a live DJ and flashing strobe lights. Teens bounce and sweat to the beat, filling the room. This is the first high school social Ryan has ever gone to. He can't believe his eyes.

Arno points out a kid wearing a sportcoat and laughs. The kid is dancing his ass off between two girls, and he looks way out of it. He's wearing women's panties on his head and twirling glow sticks in a party fever.

"Let's go to the Hip-Hop room!" Arno screams in Ryan's ear above the high decibels.

Ryan nods and motions for Arno to lead the way. He casually searches among the partiers for a raven-haired beauty as the three of them enter a second room; this one with a disco ball and a slower, but no less sweaty, atmosphere. The dancing here seems more like grinding. Yellow and white balloons are taped along the walls and streamers hang from the ceiling. Someone in the costume of Libby, the school mascot eagle, is in the middle of a dance circle doing its version of the C-walk.

"What do you want to drink?" Arno asks Ryan.

"Just get me a beer."

"This is high school. How about an energy drink?"

"That sounds tits."

"Alright. We're gonna get something. You gonna be here?"

"I might walk around," Ryan says.

Arno heads to the dry bar with Abby in tow. Ryan catches Libby getting blasted by a thrown beverage from someone in the crowd. Libby's permanent smile contrasts comedically with its angry pantomiming, brushing the soda from its feathers and refusing to dance anymore. Some of the students around try and goad it to entertain them some more, to no avail.

Ryan fights through the crowded dancing and spots Mallory almost immediately, as she walks with a group of girls on their way into a third room. Her radiating charm hits him like an elephant goring his chest. He follows the girls into the cafetorium, which is drenched in orange lighting and playing industrial rock. Mallory and her friends are at this room's bar waiting for beverages. *Be an eagle.*

He taps Mallory on the shoulder and she turns around with a smile on her face, but a lack of recognition in her eyes. "You did a good job here," Ryan yells in her ear above the loud atmosphere.

"Oh, thank you."

Ryan shows his winningest smile and nods at his accepted compliment. He bends over to yell in her ear again. "You want to dance?"

Mallory sticks her bottom lip out in exaggerated sadness. "Sorry, I don't dance."

One of Mallory's friends hands her a cola and gives Ryan a nasty look.

"Maybe my friend Trisha wants to? Hey Trish!" Mallory calls across the dance floor.

Ryan looks for the girl Mallory is summoning and flinches in disgust when he spots the fattest wildebeest ever to wear pirate boots miming back at Mallory. Mallory points at Ryan and Trisha swings her mass to face him. The beast gives a thumbs down and waves Mallory away. *Dissed by a monster. Are you kidding me?*

Mallory is dragged away by her cock-blocking friends. Ryan doesn't know what to do. He just stands there, watching the group of girls go into the basketball-court-turned-Hip-Hop room and get lost among the crowd.

"That was ineffective. Bitc–" Ryan is shoulder-bumped from behind, causing him to stumble forward. He whips around angrily, ready to throw a punch, but it's only Kerry.

"You shit-tooth," Ryan says in recognition.

"What's up?" Kerry coughs into his palm. "Thought you weren't coming."

"I just wanted to see some fern gully." Ryan shrugs. "You sell any pills?"

Kerry casts a look sideways in a conspicuous attempt to appear inconspicuous. "I made like thirty bucks. But the night is young."

"You got that gas money you owe me?"

Kerry makes a hacking laugh and wheezes, "Get a job."

Ryan waves Kerry away. "Jobs are for suckers." Someone grabs Ryan roughly from behind.

"What are you doing in here?" demands Doyle. "How'd you get inside?"

Ryan looks around for help, but Kerry has vanished.

"Come on now, Ryan. You are out!"

Ryan doesn't put up a fight as he is led out of the school social. Doyle tries to give Ryan a little push to emphasize the banishment, but only manages to thrust Ryan's shoulder forward a bit. Ryan straightens his shirt with a glare at Doyle and Rollo before he gets in his car and starts it up. He sits in his car listening to the muffled thumping coming from behind the cafetorium walls. *This was an enormous debacle.* He switches on the radio, but then quickly turns the dial away from the station playing Leila in order to find something not irritating.

As soon as he shifts into drive, Mallory comes out of the cafetorium in a rush. That asshole Lennox is chasing after her and yelling his head off.

"Get back here you trick!"

Mallory slaps against the passenger side window of Ryan's car. He unlocks the door for her and she hops in.

"Ryan?" Lennox is stunned. "You *piece* of *shit!*"

"Let's go," whimpers Mallory. She hits the lock down, stopping Lennox from clawing the door open.

Ryan picks up his jaw, watching Lennox curse at them both and pound on the window.

"Come on!" Mallory insists.

Ryan slams on the gas and burns a giant black mark on the sidewalk as he peels away. Lennox is thrown to the ground and Ryan rejoices as he spots Lennox in the rearview get up and try to stumble after.

"Wow, he is pissed. What were you doing with that asshole?"

Mallory is checking herself in the vanity mirror. "Lennox?"

"I hate that guy."

"We go out sometimes." She looks at Ryan and asks, "Do you know him?"

Ryan doesn't know what to say. *You go out sometimes?*

"I'm sorry for bothering you," she apologizes. "My name's Mallory."

"Yeah, we met."

Mallory wrinkles her eyebrows in confusion.

"In the media center," says Ryan. She still looks clueless. "I just asked you to dance."

"What's your name?"

Ryan blinks hard. "Ryan."

"Hm. I think I remember you. So what do you do, Ryan?" she asks.

"Do? I'm up for anything, I guess."

Mallory laughs softly. "No, I mean…um…do you have a job?"

"Oh." Ryan clears his throat. "Not right now. I'm in between jobs. You know how it is. I got some prospects though. Something in automotive. What about you?"

"No," Mallory says, glumly staring out the window, "but I'm going to cosmetology school when I graduate. In California, I hope. LA or somewhere around there. They have good schools over there."

"Oh yeah? You'd be good at that."

She smiles at him. "You're nice, Ryan."

Ryan swoons at her beauty. *She smells so good.* His pants get a little tighter, and it becomes slightly more difficult to drive. "I guess I should take you home?"

"To your house?" Mallory says playfully.

"Ha ha. I wish."

"I grant wishes," she says a little more playfully.

Ryan's face is burning and his chest aches with desire, but he remembers he has Jeffrey in his room and he doesn't want to blow his chances if she's not into that–not to mention that it is rude to kick out your friend just to kiss some dame. "Yeah well what I mean is, you know, I *would*, but I have a...roommate."

"Company, huh?" Mallory seems disappointed.

"Anyone at your place?" he asks hopefully.

"My parents. And my dog. We could go to the park or something. To hang out?" Mallory's phone starts ringing from her purse.

"That's closed now." Ryan cringes at the complications. His mind races with ideas on where to go. Ideas are thrown out of his mind faster than he can think of them.

Mallory closes the phone after checking the ID. "I guess it's a hassle. Just drop me off at my house," Mallory says with a yawn. "I'm tired anyway."

Ryan pulls in front of Mallory's home on Green Meadow Lane. It's a well-to-do neighborhood, all the large houses behind long driveways and perfectly maintained lawns.

He spots a Lexus in the open garage; it matches the neighbor's Mercedes. He watches Mallory adoringly as she unfastens her seat belt and unlocks the door. He doesn't want her to get away so easily.

"Can I see you again?" he asks her.

"Of course," she responds with a smile, "but I have school."

Ryan nods, unsure of whether she's brushing him off. Mallory leans in to Ryan and he tries to share a soft kiss with her. She wants a little more, and kisses him shortly, but passionately, with mostly tongue, as if she wants to eat his mouth with her lips. She leaves him stunned and with a wink, exits the car, and goes inside her house. Ryan swallows and licks her messy drool from his lips. *She tastes like blueberry muffins, too.* He starts heading home. Another successful mission. *Yeah...Where eagles dare.*

INTERROGATION ROOM 2

23

DETECTIVE MCCREADY'S WORK IS NEVER DONE. Cases keep piling on top of his desk in a constant flow. If there was no officer at the time of a crime, they sometimes take a month to make any arrest–if ever–despite eyewitnesses and having a good idea of the perp. You have to make sure that all the ducks are in a line before charging anyone, if you want to prosecute successfully anyway. Meanwhile, the criminals are walking around free and his work isn't finished.

He picks up the file marked 'Neil, Jeffrey C.' and opens it up for the umpteenth time. He'd already done a little investigating on the street, questioning his web of informants and stopping by some of the usual group of miscreants. None of his eyes and ears had a glimmer of useful information. No luck on Sapps' satanic cult theory either. And the Jalisco's beer can that that wild man with the missing ear had found turned up zilch also. The owner had just died, so obviously couldn't offer any help, and the security cameras installed turned out to be dummy. Leadless cases frustrate McCready like underwear that never stops bunching up around your bits, but he's learned to be patient. Sometimes you just have to wait. Something will pop up, usually when you least expect.

"Reeves!" McCready calls to a young Adonis officer who was ambling in his visual area.

Reeves appears annoyed, but ready for an order. "Yes sir?"

"Can you come with me to round up some of the usual for this case here? I haven't seen Pyle around."

Reeves draws back in confusion. "The grave robbery?"

"Yeah. What is it?"

"Sapps told me he's got that solved."

"What the hell are you talking about?"

Reeves blinks. "He's with a suspect right now. Working on a confession."

This information stuns McCready, and he can feel his face start to heat up with rage. *That piece of shit is trying to solve a case without me. Interrogating a suspect!* "Take me to him," he orders Reeves.

Reeves leads him down to Interrogation Room 2, but McCready stops Reeves from opening the door. "Let's go into the observation room first." They go a little further down to enter a room adjacent to the interviewing room, where McCready can see what's happening through the two-way mirror. McCready gets even more irate when he sees Sapps sitting across from a handcuffed Fancy Jack Clancy. McCready motions Reeves to hit the switch for the mic and with a press of a button, the conversation from the other room comes in over the speakers.

"–six counts of grand larceny, see?" Fancy is yelling at Sapps from his seat.

Sapps is rubbing his head and looks more than a little worn out.

"You are always accusing Fancy Jack Clancy of other things. Mindless, brainless, thoughtless things! I got some convictions, see? And suddenly, I'm guilty of everything! I do nothing but struggle to saturate this community, to make this environment a healthier, happier, and family-friendly setting! So I've got a record. So what? Robbery! Assault with a deadly weapon! Excessive speeding! Contributing to the delinquency–"

"Let's get to the point Fancy," Sapps groans.

"Not fancy, ignoramus, fanCEE! Ignoramus! You're ignorant!"

"You say you saw some kid carryin' a dead body around at a party."

"Yeah, cyborg! He disrespected me! If I ever see him, I'll tear his guts out and wear 'em like suspenders!"

"You expect me to believe that not a *single* person from this alleged party has come forward to report this? Why don't you tell me what you know? The truth."

"The truth is you're decrepit beyond all belief! The truth is you look about to die! You're ineffectual, effeminate, and flaccid! You've got low sperm count and erectile dysfunction! You're rhinoceros dung! Human slime! See? You look ready to die!"

"You already said that."

"Well now you're hearing it again! See? See? The redundancy! The repetition!"

"This is just terrific," McCready says sarcastically as he continues to observe.

"Maybe it's time you go back to your cell," Sapps threatens.

"To hell with you sucker! I know my rights, see? I'm not gonna take any guff from you! Your chatter! You want to sully me? I didn't do squat! See? Nothing!"

"I think you know somethin'. You're protectin' somebody, maybe yourself. Maybe some broad."

"You're so wrong! So perversely and academically wrong! Diametrically wrong! I'm not gonna make this into a mockery! A circus! I'm not gonna let you dictate my actions, you colossal anthropoid bottom feeding mongoloid spitlicker! See? You look disconcerted when I use all these words. Are you perplexed by the vernacular. Vocabulary!"

"It sounds like you're makin' them up."

"Isn't mongoloid a word? Retard! Isn't diametric a word, cyborg?"

McCready turns to Reeves. "Bring Pyle in here." McCready adds, "You stay in there," as Reeves is almost out the door. Through the mirror, McCready watches Reeves enter the interrogation room.

"Who's this?" Fancy asks. "Is this the interpreter? That's a delightful thing, see?"

Reeves bends over to whisper in Sapps' ear. Sapps turns to look at the mirror.

"Tell this zero that he has feces in his aorta! Feces!" Fancy is yelling. "His ventricles are covered in bile–"

McCready shuts off the audio feed. He can't stand another word from that loud mouth. Sapps gets up and walks out of the interrogation room.

"What's up McCready?" Sapps greets with a smile as he enters the observation room. "I'm about to crack this case."

"I'm about to crack your god damn skull, Pyle!" McCready explodes.

Sapps' face falls from McCready's hot words.

"What do you think you are doing?"

"I'm questionin' a suspect!" Sapps fires back. "What does it look like I'm doing?"

"It looks like you're pulling your tallywacker! How long has this been going on?"

"Two days."

McCready can't believe it. "Two fucking days?! Are you insane? You've got shit for brains!"

"I've taken enough of that abuse from him," Sapps says defensively. "I'm not takin' any from you."

"I outta kick your ass. This is not how we solve crimes around here."

"He knows somethin'—"

"He doesn't know dick! I want you to get him out of here and then I want you to get out of here. I don't want to see your fucking goofy face! If I do, I'm gonna light you up with my taser until you shit sparks!"

Reeves opens the door to the observation room and pauses, bowing his head to avoid incurring any spillage of wrath. He clears his throat before saying softly, "He says he's ready to confess."

McCready's fury goes beyond the tenth level as a satisfied smile spreads across Sapps' face.

24

RYAN IS WALKING AROUND CAMPUS WITH NEW EYES, carrying a ragged spiral notebook he has drawn all over. It's a new day and he feels like he is almost a new person. He moves with a regal air about him, purposefully, while busy students scurry about. It's a Zen moment. The air is clean. The world is bright and full of possibility. He smiles at a freckle-faced freshman girl and she smiles back, blushing. Ryan feels like a king.

He walks through the white and yellow halls of Independence High looking inside classrooms. The bell hasn't rung yet for sixth period to begin, but they are starting to seat. Ryan spots Mallory sitting in a classroom next to the desert garden and decides to go inside. She is leafing through her textbook and doesn't immediately notice Ryan take the empty seat next to her.

"What class is this?" Ryan asks her.

Her mouth works for a startled moment before she blurts, "What are you doing?"

"I came to learn something."

"I don't think this—"

The teacher, a man in his early thirties with darting eyes, bad posture, and wearing a very busy silk shirt, enters the room as the bell sounds. He stands at the front of the room and digs through his briefcase on top of his desk. Mallory mouths 'What are you doing here?' to Ryan.

"Good afternoon class," the teacher whines with the hint of a lisp. The students' response is barely audible. The teacher daintily takes a folder from his briefcase before placing it next to the white board that's situated at the front. With a small sigh, the teacher casually half-sits on his desk to face the class. "Okay people, let's get to it. Does everyone have his or her assignments ready?" He notices Ryan in the class. "Hello. Who are you?"

"Ryan."

"Well...*Ryan*...are you...in the right place?"

"Of course," Ryan replies. He can see the teacher arguing in his own mind, possibly searching for a comeback question. Ryan attempts to solve this problem early. "Mr. Jenkins transferred me here. You know him? So, I've been transferred."

"Mister Jenkins?" the teacher speaks slowly, trying to recollect. "Do you have a note?"

"Absolutely." Ryan flips through his tattered notebook like he's searching for said note. He looks around where he's sitting and checks his pockets. "It's around here..."

"Okay...um...Ryan? How about after class?"

"I wonder where I put that."

The teacher returns to addressing the full class. "Well everybody, did you enjoy the homework? I hope you had fun with the exercise, and maybe learned a little."

Only a couple groans from the students answer the teacher.

"To catch you up, Ryan, the class was assigned…um…everyone was to find a song. A theme song for themselves that describes them. Who they *are*. Understand? Oh, I'm interested in what you guys came up with! Did you people find some good ones?"

Ryan looks over at Mallory, who is paying full attention to the teacher and has her assignment neatly in front of her. Her paper is entitled 'Show You Mine'.

"Who wants to present theirs first?" the teacher asks, clasping his hands. "Did you do the assignment, Shawn?"

"Yea."

The teacher motions Shawn to proceed.

"Yea, uh, I picked *G-Lovin' Honeys* by my boy J Kewl."

"Uh-huh. Why is that?"

"I don't know. It just speaks to me. It's like what I'm all about, you know what I'm sayin'? Straight gangsta."

"Well good. That's really good. Interesting." The teacher nods as if in deep thought. It doesn't appear that he is familiar with J Kewl's artistic work so he is anxious to move forward. "How about you, Amy?"

The teacher has called on a nervous looking girl in pigtails. She has her head down over her paper and speaks softly, "I chose *Just A Boy-Toy* by The Prussians."

"Oh I love that song!" the teacher claps excitedly and attempts to sing a couple lines. "I'm just a boy-toy, just a boy-toy of joy!"

Amy continues to read softly from her paper. "The Prussians was the group Leila Caverns belonged to before she went on to pursue a solo career. This song was released on the band's debut album." Amy continues staring down at her desk, but is evidently done presenting her homework.

"Now, what made you choose this song, Amy?"

Amy just shrugs her shoulders.

"Don't know?" the teacher looks at Amy hopefully for a moment before realizing Amy has nothing further to say. "Okay. That's good. Very good, Amy." The teacher continues smiling like he believes he'll really learn something about his students through this assignment. "Alright. Who's next?" He points at Charles, the fat doorman from the school social, who is caught mid-bite while eating a candy bar. "You. Charles." The teacher points with both hands. "What did you pick? What is *your* song?"

Charles takes a second to chew his chocolate and responds, "My song? Yeah, it's Sabbath's *Iron Man*."

"Really? You think you're Iron Man?"

Charles nods. "That's what they tell me."

The teacher titters in his hands. "Are you sure it's not *I Want Candy*? By Bow Wow Wow?"

The class laughs, but none louder than Ryan. Charles shifts in his seat in embarrassment and gives the teacher a scathing look to try and save face.

In the midst of the laughter, the classroom door opens, and in comes a late student: Lennox.

"Mr. Lenny," the teacher whines with annoyance. "Are you late for this class, or are you early for the next?"

Ryan guffaws at Lennox's position. Lennox does a double-take when he sees Ryan in the class, but his sneer darkens even more when he notices Ryan is sitting next to Mallory. Lennox and Ryan are locked in a staring match of hatred.

"Here's my pass, teach." Lennox hands the teacher a slip of paper. Then, without taking his eyes from Ryan, he moves slowly to the back of the room and takes a seat.

"Who signed this?" the teacher asks Lennox while studying the pass.

"Some old crone in the office."

The teacher lays the pass on his desk. "Do you have your assignment, Lenny?" the teacher asks.

Lennox breaks his stare with Ryan. "Yeah, I do."

"Good. Well, Charlie was just saying that his theme was *I Want Candy*. What was yours?"

"No I wasn't," Charles mumbles.

"Yeah, uh," Lennox rifles through his binder while the teacher and class watch expectantly. "Jeez, I can't find it."

"Surely you have to remember. Just tell us the name of your theme song."

"Just A Boy-Toy," Ryan blurts out to some good laughs from the class.

Lennox's face turns as red as Russian morning. "Blow me, you piece of shit!"

"Lenny!" The teacher gives Lennox a stern look before turning to Ryan. "Okay, new kid. You seem to be catching on. What is your song?"

"Well," Ryan spreads his hands, "there are so many."

"Pick one."

"How 'bout that song, uh, *Keep on Rockin' in the Free World*."

"*Rocking in The Free World*?" The teacher taps his lips. "By Neil Young?"

"I wouldn't know."

"You're a clown," Lennox says from the back of the room.

"Because why?" asks the teacher, ignoring Lennox. "How would that be your song?"

"Self-explanatory. I'm keeping it rockin'," Ryan smiles at himself, "in the free world."

"Not after I kill you," Lennox barks.

"I'll kill *you*," Ryan says back.

Lennox stands up from his desk. "You want some?"

"Anytime, turkey."

"Gentlemen!" the teacher tries to control the situation. "This is getting out of hand. Lenny, sit down."

"Sit down, Lenny," Ryan mocks.

Lennox tosses his desk over in a rage and leaps at Ryan, who is still sitting. They crash to the floor and Lennox is choking the life out of Ryan.

"What are you doing here!?" Lennox screams. "What are you doing with my girl!?"

Ryan's face starts turning purple. The teacher is frantic and the other students are out of their seats laughing and cheering. Charlie and an over-dressed student pull Lennox from Ryan.

"Get out of my classroom!" the teacher screeches at Lennox. "Go see Principal Adams. Right now! You're getting a referral."

Ryan collects himself calmly and brushes his shirt straight. He sets his desk back up a little closer to Mallory's and puts his arm around her. "Not too smart, guy."

Lennox makes another attempt at throwing himself at Ryan, but is held back by Charles.

The teacher points at Charles in a huff. "Charlie, you go with him. Make sure he goes to Principal Adam's office directly!"

Charles grips Lennox's shoulder, but Lennox swats the hand off immediately. "Don't touch me, you fat turd." Charles follows Lennox out of the class.

"Okay...my god!" The teacher takes a seat at his desk, fanning himself and breathing deeply in an attempt to calm his nerves. "Such...unusual...behavior. Settle down class." The teacher seems to be the only one having a tough time settling down. The students are all back in their seats, the interest from the momentary spectacle gone. "Where were we?" The bell chimes, signaling the end of the period, and the teacher exhales in relief. "Thank you. Saved, it seems."

The students are already funneling out of the room.

Ryan follows Mallory outside and joins her as she walks to her next class.

"So why were you here?" she asks him. "I hope it's not because of me."

"There's lots of reasons. I was feeling I needed to brush up on my, uh, Math, and...what class was that?"

"Ethics."

Ryan laughs. "They let that guy teach ethics?"

"What do you mean, *that* guy?"

"He's a raging twinkle-toes."

"You know, you're pretty rude."

Ryan grabs her by the arm and they stop in the hallway. He decides honesty might pay off here. "I did want to see you again."

She looks at him with a little smirk, but shakes her head slightly. "I don't know."

"Come on. Let's get out of here," he entices.

"What, right now? I have two more classes left."

"Ditch 'em."

"You're a naughty boy, aren't you?" she says, with a glint in her eye. "Where do you want to go?"

Ryan hadn't thought that far ahead. "Your room."

"Mm, my room, huh?" Mallory bites her lip coyly. "Okay."

Ryan surges with excitement.

"But after school," she quickly adds.

"Yeah?"

"I'll be there at three-thirty, and my parents don't get back till about six."

"I'll see you there." Ryan waves goodbye.

"Don't you have more classes?" she asks in puzzlement.

"I think I learned enough for today."

25

WITH DARKNESS AT HIS SIDE, A MAN WITH A FACE
so gaunt he looks like a skeleton opens the door to U.S. Auto
UnLTD like a cowboy entering a saloon. He coolly looks the place
over from behind his dark sunglasses while standing in the doorway,
inhaling the store's fragrance as if he were smelling the divine odor
of a home-cooked meal. Fresh rubber, motor greases, plastics, and
pine fresheners. A scent unique to stores like this, albeit a mellowed
version of a real mechanic's garage, but the man in black momentarily
retains it in his lungs.

Unfortunately, the store corrupts the mood by piping some
pop music into the air through its PA system, along with public
announcements of current sales.

A nappy-haired clerk is working at her station, ringing up some
items for a pregnant woman, but she is captivated at the sight of this
road warrior silhouetted in the doorway. She eyes the man with the
mangled ear as he makes a beeline for the octane boost. He grabs a
bottle with his sinewy left hand, opens it, places his thumb over the
spout and turns the bottle over. He rubs the little liquid dab between
his fingers and touches it to his tongue. Satisfied, he replaces the cap
and takes it to the counter.

The clerk manages to finish ringing in the pregnant woman despite being distracted by the raw energy vibes–like invisible rays of black sunshine–surrounding the tall skeletal man. The pregnant woman leaves with a sideways glance at the spooky character, and the clerk scans the octane boost into the register.

"I'm looking for a car," he begins, in a voice like the soft grind of a blade carving in stone. "Brown. Four-door sedan. Probably... early eighties. Maybe a St. Regis or Newport. Have you seen anyone come in here with a car like that?"

"Have I seen a brown car?" she wheezes.

"It's driven by a hot-rodder punk," the man continues, emotionless. "A teenager who drives way too fast."

The clerk appears clueless. Her attention turns to a lazy-eyed man that gets in the checkout line. The man, who looks like a bum, has his arms full of custom accessories, floor mats, decals, and other useless junk.

"See it's him I want," the man goes on, bringing the clerk's mind back to him. "Forget the car. It's a jalopy anyway." He tries to simplify the situation. "He's got something, and I need to take it from him."

"Yeah, sorry. Really not sure, hun. Maybe the police can help you find your car? You should try them, I guess." The clerk smiles over the bald man's shoulder to the lazy-eyed guy who dumps his items on the counter. She starts ringing in the products, avoiding the man in jet.

In one fluid motion, stone-faced behind his opaque glasses, he pulls out his Double Eagle pistol with his bony right hand, the blue, green, and yellow flashing down his arm under his black coat, and points the pistol at the lazy-eyed customer's head.

The customer raises his arms in the air as high as they'll go: the clerk's jaw drops. Then, striking with the deathly nature of a scorpion's sting, the grim man swings the pistol around at the computer register and blows it to pieces with a deafening spray of glass and sparks.

The clerk hits the ground with a thud as she passes out from fear.

"Have you seen a male teen driving a brown eighties sedan?" the tall skeletal man asks the stunned customer levelly. The customer shakes his head slightly, his lazy eyes wide. The man wearing night takes his octane boost and leaves. "This town is a bunch of morons."

26

A DIFFERENT VIEW

"..."

27

"I'M GOING TO PUT THIS IN MY ROOM," MALLORY SAYS about her backpack as Ryan follows her into her home. She goes off down a hallway to do this, leaving him alone in the entryway. The first room is some sort of socializing area painted in a light peach color except for the vaulted pearl white ceiling that matches the carpeted floor. *Should I take my shoes off?* Ryan wonders, observing how the dark wood furniture is neatly arranged like a catalogue photo. Every little accessory, including fake fruit on the coffee table, is specifically placed and organized. It even smells like potpourri. All of the cleanliness and order makes Ryan slightly uncomfortable, but he shrugs it off. *Screw it. Let's see what we can find.*

He walks into the living room, tracking dirt on the floor, and spots a mini-bar with sophisticated etched glass bottles and glassware. "Don't mind if I do," Ryan says gleefully as he pours himself a highball from a decanter that looks like whiskey. On the mantle next to the bar is a framed photo of the ugliest little dog he has ever seen. Ryan picks up the picture and laughs at it. The dog looks like it has a disease. Its hair is falling out in large patches, revealing reddish splotchy skin, and it has a tail that looks like a giant rat's.

This thing is hideous, Ryan laughs to himself while taking a big drink from his glass. His face turns sour, contorting with disgust like he just took a sip from a cockroach smoothie. He lets the liquid dribble from the side of his mouth and spits it back into the bottle.

"What are you doing?" Mallory asks.

"What is this?" Ryan demands, wiping his mouth.

"It's just colored water," she giggles. "Both of my parents are alkies."

"That's a dirty trick."

"Well my mother is the original fashion whore. She would never get rid of her good crystal. You shouldn't just go around in other people's homes making yourself comfortable, anyway. What if that was poison?"

"Poison?" Ryan feels a little feverish.

"Relax. You got lucky this time." With a light laugh, Mallory takes Ryan by the hand. "I got the real stuff in my room. Come on."

She leads him to her bedroom, decorated in a pink motif and cushioned with frilly pillows and stuffed animals. Numerous dolls are placed around on shelves, dressers, and her bed. A poster of a male underwear model–with his stuff on the verge of popping out–clashes with the innocent girlie décor. Her mirror is outlined with photos of her partying with friends. Ryan is a little agitated to see Lennox in a few of the photos, but it looks like there are plenty of other guy friends photographed with Mallory. Ryan just tries to cast this out of his mind while Mallory pops the new Leila CD into her stereo and turns it on for background music.

Ryan leans against the toy chest, trying to make himself at ease, and Mallory stretches herself along the width of her bed.

"I thought you had the real stuff in here," Ryan says.

Mallory bounces to her feet and pulls a bottle from underneath. "Yeah, I got some. You want me to mix you a drink?"

"Sure. Please."

Mallory pours the contents of the bottle into a tall flower vase she uses like a pimp chalice and hands it to Ryan, then gets back on the fluffy bed. Ryan takes a little sip from the vase cocktail.

"Mm," Ryan inhales in an attempt to cool his mouth, "that's super good."

"Is it?"

"Yeah," he lies. Ryan smacks his lips a little to show he finds it tasty. "A little tart." He lets his eyes wander around the room some more, soaking it in. *This is the greatest place on Earth.*

"Do you play any instruments?" Mallory asks him.

"The guitar," he answers. "Well, I used to."

"Not anymore?"

"Not for awhile. I broke a couple strings," he explains, "I guess from jamming too hard, so it's been a couple years."

"Oh." Mallory gets up from the bed and picks up a book of matches that were set next to a large candle labeled 'Blueberry Dreams'. She strikes a match and lights it, placing the used match in the dish holding the candles runoff. The ceramic dish is coated in a thick layer of melted blue wax. "I love this candle," she tells him. "It smells sooooo good."

Ryan doesn't know what to say. He can't help but feel he has become part of some ritual. Mallory climbs back on her bed like a cat with its tail in the air.

"I went shopping yesterday," she purrs.

"Oh yeah?" Ryan feigns interest as he tries to memorize her languid movements in glimpses.

Mallory pulls down her skirt enough to show off her black thong panties. Ryan notices that she has no tan lines. He notices he has finished half the drink she served him. He wipes a small–very small–bit of perspiration from his forehead.

"And a matching top, too."

"Yeah?" Ryan is no longer faking interest in Mallory's shopping exploits. He swallows hard, trying to regain moisture in his mouth.

Mallory lies on her bed with her head and hair falling off the edge. She looks at Ryan with a sly smile. "You want to be my boyfriend, don't you?"

Ryan doesn't know how to answer this. Her scent fills his mind, sending it spinning. It spins faster as she unbuttons her blouse to reveal her large perky and supple breasts. Ryan takes a large drink from the vase while studying her exposed flesh, his eyes, as open as possible and unblinking, trying to burn the image into his corneas. He cautiously sets the drink down and joins Mallory on the bed.

28

MCCREADY LET SAPPS GET THE PAPERWORK READY for a signed confession. Evidently, Fancy is willing to sign a full confession detailing how and why he robbed the grave, including the current whereabouts of the corpse. Of course Fancy's had a few little demands: a tub of pomade, a fruitcup sans melon, and a small radio. They seemed easy enough, and as long as they keep him complacent and manageable, McCready doesn't care. But Fancy is still delaying signing the confession and is unwilling to have it recorded on tape.

As McCready walks the halls of the Everdale Police Department, he can't help but wonder why he is going along with this farce. It seems unlikely that Fancy is the culprit in this case, but if he's willing to confess, that frees up time for other cases. Waiting on his desk is a purse snatching, hit and run, and credit fraud. Much more important. Still, he prefers to do everything the right way and just doesn't feel a hundred percent about tagging this crime on Fancy.

He approaches Interrogation Room 2 where Sapps and Fancy are waiting for him to bring today's demand for a copy of the latest edition of the men's entertainment magazine CREASE. He can hear Fancy screaming from a mile away. McCready takes a deep breath before entering the room.

"Here he is!" Fancy cheers, bouncing out of his seat. "The grand wizard! The mastermind! You here to see the prince? Me! The boss? Take a look! Bask in the resplendence!"

"You look worse than ever," McCready says honestly.

"You kidding me? You gutless coward!"

"Alright Fancy," Sapps says. "McCready is here with your porno, so let's do this."

"I don't care! He could be the President of the United States! I don't give two shits or a fuck! See? He's maggot custard and you're a fistful of flatulence!"

"You said you'd sign this if we got what you wanted and we held up our side!" McCready yells. "You think you can change your mind?"

"I say suck and you say how hard, see? I'm calling it! I'm in charge here, see? Because you're riff-raff! Leftovers! Debris!"

"Come on Fancy. Let's just finish this," Sapps pleads.

"You got to annunciate when you're talkin' to me!"

"Let's finish this."

"I can't hear you! You're all garbled! You got to annunciate when you say your pieces and things, see? You sound like a mealy-mouthed ninny! A–"

"God damn you Fancy! We're not givin' you anythin' else!"

"Pardon me! I'm talking here! My speech, see? I'm talking! Don't interrupt me ever, chump chimp baboon! That was just an additional decoy! A subterfuge! Another obviation of time because that's my way! That's how I prefer to do it! See? If I prefer to sign a confession, I will!"

"Here it is!" Sapps presents the papers and pen.

"Cyborg! Can you turn your circuitry to mute!? Can you do me that courtesy? I said *if* I prefer to do it, I didn't say I did prefer to do it that way, see? I'm mystifying!"

"What's it goin' to take?' Sapps seems ready to melt after spending all this toxic time around Fancy.

"What's it going to take, you ask? You'll do whatever it demands?"

"Just sign this confession."

"So basically I could, I could suckle on you, reach-around on you, twist off all over you?! Or I could defecate on your tombstone?!"

"You can twist the night away. Right after you sign this."

Fancy laughs. "How wonderful! Where do I begin?"

"Just tell us what happened. What you did," McCready says.

Fancy inhales deeply, looking from McCready to Sapps. He folds his hands together and stares at them as he begins somewhat solemnly, "I was fixing him. Tyson style! I was biting him, see? I even tore a chunk and spit it out, see? I did whatever I could, but he kept coming!"

"Who?" McCready asks.

"Shut up, shit spritz!" Fancy slaps his hand on the table. "I'm talking here! I'm talking!"

McCready throws his hands in the air and Fancy Jack continues in his usual temper.

"I told him it wasn't my fault—just an accident! I told him to take the money! And he did! He said he'd be back. When the money could no longer buy time. We have an appointed fate. Fear is just a different death!" Fancy is practically screaming at the top of his lungs. "Don't you see?!"

"What the hell are you talking about?"

"Just follow it for a few minutes, human excrement!"

"Where does the corpse come in here?"

"Do you happen to speak French?" Fancy asks McCready.

"No."

"Evidently you don't understand English! You thankless diabetic!"

McCready grabs the confession documents. "You know what, schmuck?"

"Don't tell me nothing! I'm telling you that right now!"

McCready signs Fancy's name to the dotted line. "Fuck you. I did it for you!"

"You can't do that," Sapps says.

"He's a loser!"

"You got nothing!" Fancy screams. "You only got what I gave you! You're a pig and this is *hog*wash! Pig shit, see?! Treachery!"

"Put him back in his cell and let him rot!" McCready tells Sapps on his way out of Interrogation Room 2.

29

RYAN FEELS CONTENT–HAPPY MAYBE–SITTING IN THE school cafetorium with Denise and Arno for a quiet lunch. He nibbles from his blueberry muffin, relishing every morsel, and studies his friends. They both look clammy, morose, sickly; like Nosferatu's children. *This is a good goddamn muffin!* Ryan contemplates his food and looks around the cafetorium while they all sit there in virtual silence. He sees a kid in a sports coat standing on top of a table chanting some gibberish Ryan can't quite make out, but the other kids around that table are laughing and cheering him on. It all seems muted from Ryan's table.

"What are you doing here, Ryan?" Denise breaks the tranquil tension bitingly. Arno spits out his food in wheezing laughter.

"Going to school!" Ryan answers. "What the hell are you doing here?"

"How many classes are you taking?" she drills.

"One."

"It's boring here," Arno rasps.

"You sick too, now?" Ryan asks. Arno nods as he tries to clear his throat. Ryan takes a bite from his delicacy and looks from Arno to Denise. "So where's Kerry?"

"He's at home," says Denise. "He's not feeling well."

"How come you don't hang out with your friends no more?" Arno asks.

Ryan looks at both of them, their puffy eyes intent on him. "What is this?"

"Where did you put that body?" Denise hisses.

"What do you care?"

Denise shifts toward Ryan suddenly, her eyes are wide, panicked. Her feral look makes Ryan's skin tingle. He scoots away. *This bitch has lost her mind!*

"Has anything," she looks around the cafetorium and lowers her voice, "been...*happening*...to you?" The hair on Ryan's neck stands up from Denise's disturbing countenance. Something isn't right, like a little voice in his head screaming ferociously and wildly in warning. But the voice disappears so fast Ryan doesn't know if it was ever really there.

The lunch bell rings. Ryan warily gets up from the table and slowly backs away from Denise. "I've got...to go...to...class." He takes a few steps from the table before turning away.

"Why are you even here, Ryan?" she screeches after him. "Why are you here!?"

RYAN WALKS INTO ETHICS CLASS TO THE SIGHT OF lennox and Mallory sitting together and talking; both are too caught up to notice him enter. And not just that, but Mallory seems…giddy. He doesn't know what to do–he's stunned–so he takes a seat in the back of the room. The bell chimes and the teacher, today in a shirt that makes the previous one look conservative, calls attention.

"Hey, everyone! Could you please excuse yourselves from talking? I want to get to some important business." The teacher sets a stack of papers on Mallory's desk and asks her to help hand them out. She seems somewhat surprised when she notices Ryan in class, but only gives him a wink as she passes him a handout entitled 'What is the importance of values and ethics in today's world?'. "You will all pair up," the teacher continues. "Look to the person next to you. They will be your partner for this project."

Ryan is in a daze. *What game is Mallory playing?* He looks to the right and sees the back of the girl's head next to him. He turns to the left and sees an overly dressed boy smiling at him with his hand extended.

"Hello my friend," the boy speaks with a heavy accent.

Ryan shakes his head in exasperation. "What the hell?"

"This is a very critical assignment," the teacher goes on.

Ryan raises his hand in the air, but before he is called on, he blurts out, "You got to be kidding me, right?"

"Excuse me?"

"Why can't we pick our own partners?"

"Because this is the best way and this is the way I do things, Mister Ryan," the teacher explains patiently.

Lennox notices Ryan watching him with Mallory, so he moves a little closer to the raven-haired beauty.

Ryan is burning up inside. *I can't let Mallory work with that guy! Why is she even talking to him?* "I don't even know what language this guy speaks," Ryan pleads his case.

"I speak English ver'well," says the boy.

"Don't you think he'd be better with the hickey machines in the corner?" Ryan gestures to a pock-faced kid that has been trying to cultivate his mustache and his fat girlfriend with large bangs.

"There will be no further discussion on this," the teacher says firmly. "Manny is your partner."

Ryan looks over at the over-dressed boy who still has his hand out.

"Hello," the boy says. "I am Manuelo."

Ryan is in hell.

* * *

A midnight red '67 Buick Riviera prowls through the Independence High parking corral like a lion on the African savannah, the gate for the lot left smashed open and swinging off its hinges. The sinister car stops behind a brown sedan.

A tall man wearing jet black gets out of the Buick, moving like a wraith as he expertly jimmies the sedan open and reaches in to pop the trunk. In the brown sedan's rear compartment is an assortment of dirty tools; a muddy shovel, pickaxe…items used for digging.

A dark cloud passes across the gaunt man's face throwing thunderbolts. He opens the trunk to his Riviera and transfers the shovel and pickaxe to his car. Rummaging a little more in the sedan's trunk, he discovers a large sledgehammer. A smile grows on the man's face as he examines the heavy tool. A crocodile smile.

* * *

Ethics class has ended and Ryan walks out, followed by his project partner, Manuelo. He stands in the desert garden outside the class and picks one of the leaves off a tree. He tears the leaf to shreds staring at the class door and lets the remnants fall to his feet.

"I always look forward to learning about the culture of United States," says Manuelo to Ryan.

"There's no culture here," Ryan dismisses. He paces in a circle, eyeing the class door.

To further fuel Ryan's dismay, Mallory and Lennox emerge together.

"See you later then?" Lennox is saying to Mallory. She says 'okay' and waves him a little goodbye as he leaves. He flips Ryan the bird as he goes, while Ryan tries to stare a hole through Lennox's back.

"Two in a row?" Mallory says to Ryan. "I didn't think you were coming back."

"You let that asshole limpdick sit next to you?" Ryan erupts.

"He's not a limpdick."

Manuelo sees it's time to go. "I will see you later, my friend."

"Take it sleazy." Ryan waves him away without looking, his eyes still on Mallory. "I thought you hated him?"

"He apologized." Mallory sees that Ryan is distraught. "He just wants to be friends anyways."

"I *hate* that guy." Ryan punches his gloved palm.

"Don't be jealous. It's so disgusting," she tells him. She leans in and kisses him, but he is unresponsive. "Why don't you come over later? For dinner?"

"Won't your parents be there?"

"You can meet them."

"Why?"

Mallory steps back from him, the muscles along her jaw tightening. "Is this going to be a problem? I didn't ask you to come here."

"Alright, alright. Dinner. Sounds great."

"That's better."

31

WHY ARE YOU EVEN HERE? DENISE'S WORDS REVERBERATE in Ryan's thoughts as he sits in his car studying himself in the rearview mirror. *Am I letting myself be played like a sucker? Does she think I'm a stupid turkey?* Ryan turns the ignition, but the car doesn't fire up. He pumps the gas and then tries again, but the engine doesn't even crank.

Ryan passively recognizes Manuelo having a smoke by his car, a blue '93 Subaru SVX, watching him struggle with starting The Defiler.

Manuelo throws down the cigarette butt and gets into his dilapidated sports car. He pulls up to Ryan who is now checking under the Newport's hood and gawking at what he sees.

"That peon asshole Lennox," Ryan weeps. "I never thought he would stoop so low. I can't believe this shit. It's unbelievable."

"Hello, my friend," Manuelo says.

"My car is completely ruined!" Ryan explodes. "The engine is all smashed to bits!" He spins on the brink of a meltdown and sobs, "The defiler...defiled."

"You need a ride?" Manuelo offers.

Ryan laughs sadly at Manuelo's dinky vehicle with ground effects and oversized spoiler. "Are you kidding me?"

"Hey, at least it runs, man," Manuelo says defensively. "You need a ride or what? You do not need to be a mother fucker."

Something catches Ryan's eye: a customized Buick Riviera drifting into the school parking, its front end like a devil's fork and body language carrying menace. It's unmistakably the same sinister car driven by the maniac from the other night. Ryan closes the Chrysler's hood and leaps into Manuelo's ride. "We need to go!"

"Sure, man. Where do you want to go?" Manuelo doesn't recognize Ryan's urgency.

"That way!" Ryan yells, pointing in the opposite direction of the approaching Buick. The Buick has realized Ryan is about to escape in the blue Subaru and squeals around the corner, attempting to not let its prey escape.

"That is a football field, my friend," says Manuelo.

"Just go!"

Manuelo jams the gas and the Subaru ramps over a curb into the Independence High soccer field. The car struggles for a moment to gain traction in the grass, throwing mud and turf everywhere. The coaches and students are yelling at them as if they've gone berserk, the Buick is at the curb choosing whether or not to enter the field.

Manuelo shifts into another gear and the Subaru romps its way across the field, through the chain fence, and out to the street on the other side. Ryan looks back and sees the Buick starting to make its way around the field instead of going across.

"We need to get out of this area fast!" Ryan says in a panic.

Manuelo zigzags through traffic like it's competitive slalom. Speeding down the street, they rapidly put distance between themselves and the school, and hopefully the psycho Buick driver.

"Hey thanks," Ryan says sincerely.

"*De nada.*"

"Where did you learn to drive like that?"

"Like what?" asks Manuelo. "I learned to drive in Mexico."

Ryan notices that Manuelo doesn't seem rattled by the getaway. He just takes everything as a normal occurrence.

Manuelo pulls a flask out of the inner console and offers it to Ryan. "You want some brandy, man?"

"Uh, thanks," Ryan says, somewhat baffled. He takes the flask and swigs from it. "Holy *shit* this is hot." Ryan cringes and hands the flask back to Manuelo who is laughing. Manuelo takes a swig and handles it like he was drinking tea.

"So we going to work on this project or what?" Manuelo asks.

"Project? Sorry essay, but I don't need to do that project."

"What do you mean?"

"I'm not even registered in that class, homie. Comprendo?"

"I do not know what you are thinking, *payaso*, but your thinking of me is not right. I do not wear a Texas hat or listen to *campesina* music. I am not like these *pinches nacos* you have here. *Soy de Querètaro, Mexico.* So do not talk to me like I am a idiot."

Ryan is thrown off by Manuelo's rant. "Sorry."

"Is okay." Manuelo points to Super Convenience UnLTD. "I have to stop real fast. You speak Spanish?"

"No."

They park and enter the store where the same greaseball clerk that rejected Ryan's ID earlier sits behind the counter. Manuelo goes right up to the guy and gives him daps.

"*¿Que onda, güey?*" Manuelo greets the clerk happily. Ryan spots Manuelo slipping the clerk a folded bill. "*Dame el 'Presidente', tambien.*"

The clerk gives Ryan the evil eye. Manuelo sees the hesitation and look from the clerk. "He is cool, man. No problem." Ryan smiles at the clerk.

"*El es un mamon,*" the clerk says, shaking his head at Ryan.

"*Sì, pero es buena onda. Seguro.*" Manuelo laughs.

The clerk nods and pulls a large bottle of Presidente from underneath the counter. Manuelo thanks the clerk and he and Ryan exit the store.

"I do not give a shit about school work either," Manuelo continues the conversation. "I came here for the pussy," Manuelo peels off a baggy filled with white powder that was taped underneath the brandy bottle, "and the good drugs."

"Rock n' roll, Manuelo," Ryan says in wonderment.

"Can we go to your place and drink this shit?"

"I insist."

"WHAT'S YOUR MALFUNCTION?" ROLLO ASKS LENNOX as they walk through the Independence High parking lot.

"Nothing!" Lennox erupts. In a fit, Lennox launches his backpack at his truck like a shot put. It almost makes it into the bed, but hits the faded and peeling 'God Bless America' sticker on the tailgate and tumbles over the edge onto the pavement with a loud thud.

Doyle makes eye contact with his brother in concern for Lennox. Rollo responds with only a shake of his head.

"That piece of shit Ryan has been seeing my girl!" Lennox continues his tantrum. "I want to strangle them both!" He gazes at his hands as if imagining the deed.

This isn't news to Rollo. He had witnessed the spectacle at the social and has also been privy to some juicy rumors concerning Mallory. "Come on Lennox, you can't let some cock-hound get under your skin. Girls like to mess with guys' minds." Rollo watches Lennox visibly try to grab a hold on his rage. "That's all."

"Piss on her," Doyle adds. "You can do better anyway."

Lennox runs his hands through his hair and takes a deep breath. "I know. I know."

"Come on. Let's go get some beer and jack some shit," Rollo says appeasingly.

"Or?" Doyle teases. He's dancing on his toes; he must have an idea.

"Spit it out, carbunkle," Rollo demands.

Doyle grins. "Or we can do something that hits Ryan where it hurts," he says, rubbing the dark bruise still on his temple from Ryan hitting him with the forty ounce.

"Like what?" Lennox asks in intrigue.

Doyle points to a crusty brown sedan parked near the back of the lot. "Ryan's beater."

Lenox smiles cruelly.

"His car? How are we supposed to hurt Ryan with it? It's a POS."

"Yeah it is," Doyle says, "but Ryan loves it. You know that."

"Yeah, it's perfect." Lennox is already sold on this scheme.

"What are we gonna do with it, genius?" Rollo asks.

"I'll take a shit right on the hood!" Lennox boasts. "Too bad it doesn't have a sunroof though."

"We steal it," is the answer. "And dump it into the town lake."

"No, I don't think so." Rollo is the voice of reason today. "You don't know how to steal a car."

"I bet you." Doyle smiles.

"Alright," Rollo takes the bet, "let's see."

Lennox is already heading towards the Chrysler Newport.

"I thought you knew how to hotwire a car. Stupid shit." Rollo stands outside of Ryan's brown Newport as a lookout while Doyle works at the steering column. Lennox sits in the passenger seat fiddling through the glove compartment junk.

"Yeah I do, dildo!" Doyle contends.

"How long are you gonna try rubbing those wires? You broke the car, jizz-breath."

"No I didn't. There's no juice." He pulls a lever at his feet to pop the hood. "Here. Check the battery cables. Or we can do it from inside if you got a screwdriver."

"Hmm, I see," Rollo says after opening the hood.

"What is it? Loose connection?"

Rollo reaches under the hood and pulls out a severed black cable; its wiring completely shredded.

Doyle gets out of the car to see under the Chrysler's hood. "Holy shit! It's all crunched up!" Doyle laughs.

"What a waste of time." Lennox digs through the glove compartment, finds a lighter and sparks it up. He adjusts the flame to a tall torch.

"Maybe we can push it into the lake?" Doyle suggests.

"I think someone beat us to the punch."

Lennox grabs a paper out of the glove compartment. "I don't think he'll need his registration anymore." He sets the paper on fire with the torch-sized flame. It goes up faster than he expected and it scorches his finger. He casts it away in pain. The burning paper falls onto other papers and soon a small fire is raging in Ryan's car. "Holy shit!"

"What the hell, fool?" Rollo says, slamming the hood shut.

The three of them run a safe distance away from the car as the fire spreads unbelievably fast. Then the whole insides catch and all at once, the car is an inferno.

"Let's get out of here!"

They back away, mesmerized by the dancing flames. Doyle squeals as the engine of the car pops in a loud burst, followed by the fuel tank exploding.

Thick black smoke billows into the sky and Rollo becomes aware of an audience starting to gather and hears sirens in the distance. "Come on! Before the cops and fire department get here!"

Hearts racing, the three climb into Lennox's lifted Chevy and escape the blazing disasterpiece.

33

MANUELO CUTS THICK LINES FROM THE BAGGY HE GOT at Super Convenience, then snorts a couple using a rolled page from CREASE magazine. His gaze lands on Jeffrey sitting in the corner of Ryan's room and he sniffs hard, rubbing his nose.

"Does he bother you?" Ryan asks.

Manuelo gives a 'who, me?' expression. "*No me importa.* We have dead people everywhere in Mexico. Dead people, cats, dogs. Once my cousin hit this dead body in the stomach with a stick."

"I've never been to Mexico. Which do you like better? Everdale really sucks, but I heard Mexico is horrible."

"Why? I love my home, man. It is very different, well, there are similarities, but I am Mexican. You only have one home."

"Similarities? What's it like compared to here?"

Manuelo scratches his head. "I see some familiar things. More people sell things on the streets where I am from. You do not have that here very much. This city does not have walls around the homes, I see. I think there is more order in your city."

Ryan nods and sips his beer. "Who do you stay with out here?"

Manuelo puts a cigarette in his mouth. "These old people. *Los Stephens.*"

"Oh yeah? How are they?"

Manuelo lights his smoke and shrugs. "It is cool, man. They do not care what I do. They get a check every month from my parents. My dad manufactures leather goods like purses and boots, so he can afford it."

"They let you have girls there?"

Manuelo laughs. "I do not know, my friend. I have not made any pussy since I got here."

"Oh."

"But I will, man," Manuelo assures. "It is different here than Mexico. Over there they are all religious and most do not do blowjobs."

"That's crap."

"Serious, man. There are many *putas* here. Girls here sex everybody."

"Hey, Manuelo, would you mind dropping me off somewhere in about an hour?"

Manuelo gets up from his seat and stretches. "Sure, man. Where?"

"You know that girl from ethics class, Mallory?" Ryan says boastfully. "She's got dark hair, pretty."

"The one with the *pechugotas!* That is good stuff man. Like I say, girls here, very different than where I come from."

Ryan beams with pride and downs the rest of his brew.

Manuelo punches the air in a fit. "Man, I feel good. You have to show me the tour here. We should go find some *mamacitas*, man!"

"I don't know Manuelo. My ride is sitting back at school. I'm pretty pissed about that. At first I thought that it was that asshole Lennox who decimated my car..." Ryan pictures the dark red Riviera from the previous night and the man trying to shoot him and then appearing again at the high school, "...but I'm not sure anymore." He regards Jeffrey warily as he fills Manuelo's flask with the Presidente brandy. Denise's warning flashes through his mind, and he takes a nip from the bottle. "I feel like breaking something."

"*Orale* man. You and I should go out. Find some girls or find trouble." Manuelo laughs and kicks at the air. "Better *los dos*."

"I got that date later."

"*¡Ay caray!* Ask her to come, man. She is welcome."

Ryan shakes his head. "It's not like that. She wants me to meet her parents."

"That sounds serious, man." Manuelo laughs in a high pitch. "Sounds like some horse shit! We have time to get a rum. Lesgo."

Ryan doesn't see why not. "Let's go, penday-ho!"

Manuelo laughs in an even higher pitch and wipes his damp hair from his forehead. "You speak Spanish already, man. We make you a Mexican tonight!"

A VOW

34

THE SUN IS ON ITS DESCENDING ARC AS MANUELO and Ryan cruise around Everdale, Manuelo weaving through traffic in his small Subaru, accelerating quickly and making abrupt stops.

"Which way to the *discoteca*, man?" Manuelo yells over the radio.

"You mean a club? You know you have to be twenty-one to get in those, right?"

"Twenty-one?" Manuelo laughs. "Serious? I will be dead by then, man. Where can we go for the women?"

"Shit, it's early. I'm not sure." Ryan takes a nip from the flask of brandy. "There might be some girls at the mall. It's hard to find anything to do here. I told you, Everdale is a vortex of ball-crushers."

"If there is girls at the mall, we go to the mall. We bring the fun, man."

"Alright. The mall. Let's stop over at Independence, so I can get some cash out of my car."

* * *

143

"Aw hell no."

"It is only a car, man," Manuelo says, referring to a blackened husk sitting in the Independence High parking lot: evidently the charred remains of Ryan's Chrysler Newport. The fire department must have been there because the car is still dripping wet. The remnants of the vehicle seem to have melted into the asphalt.

"Aw heeeell no," Ryan says again as he walks around the crisped car. He tries to open a door, but it is welded shut.

"At least you were not hurt," Manuelo consoles. He lights up another smoke and takes a deep puff. "Drink this, man." Manuelo hands Ryan the flask.

"Whoever did this must pay," Ryan vows and seals the promise with a long drink of brandy. "Screw it. Let's hit the mall."

CHARM

RYAN IS STILL IN A FOG OF LAMENTATION FOR THE cremains of his hobby cruiser as he and Manuelo enter the West Everdale Mall through the automatic sliding doors. The West Everdale Mall is one of the five big malls in Everdale, and in Ryan's opinion, the only difference between the shopping centers is the location. They all offer the same merchandise at the same prices, and they are all riddled with old people.

"Do you have places like this in Mexico?" he asks Manuelo as he grabs the flask of brandy from him and takes a swig. He thinks he may be experiencing shock, and he is unsure if the reality of his destroyed car has sunk in. He feels bereft of all emotion, but he thinks the brandy may be helping. He puts the flask in his pocket.

"Yeah, man," Manuelo says. "We have places just like this." Manuelo lights up a cigarette as the two walk through a department store to get into the general mall area.

* * *

Lennox, accompanied by Rollo and Doyle, is in DD's Jewelry Store UnLTD., where the clerk girl is showing him a charm bracelet. "This is the fashion now?" he asks.

"Oh, yes," the girl says. "It's very popular among the ladies now. Your girlfriend will love it."

Doyle and Rollo are trying on some women's sunglasses and laughing at each other's look.

"I thought that was you," Ryan says as he walks into the jewelry store. "Check these tards out, Manuelo. Coming out of the closet, Rollo?"

Rollo snatches the Liberace shades off his face. "Stick it!"

"You can't smoke in here," the clerk scolds Ryan's friend.

The friend stays close to the doorway, but doesn't put out his cigarette.

"What do you want?" Lennox asks with venom.

"I just wanted to make sure my eyes weren't deceiving me. And I see they weren't. You're still an ugly jackfuck." Ryan looks at the charm held in the shop girl's hand. "It suits you perfectly," he tells Lennox.

"It's not for me," Lennox snaps.

"Man!" Ryan's friend exclaims. He's pointing out the window at some chicks riding the escalator to the lower level of the mall. "Did you see those women? Come on, I must talk with them." He is already out the door in hot pursuit.

Lennox just smirks at Ryan who is now alone and outnumbered. "Nice company you keep, Ryan. You wad."

"Yeah? Thanks." Ryan slowly backs out of the store. "Have fun diddling yourselves."

"What a wimp," Doyle remarks.

"I *hate* that guy," Lennox states, punching his knuckles together.

"So do you want it?" the clerk asks about the charm.

"What's your return policy?" he asks her.

* * *

Manuelo has caught up to these two young girls across from the bookstore advertising an upcoming appearance by the author of the new release *Rust, Wheat, and Beige: The American Reality*. Ryan walks up to them, making sure he appears in no hurry.

"This is my friend Ryan," Manuelo introduces.

They all say hi to each other.

"Where are you from?" one of the girls asks Manuelo as she twirls her necklace around her finger.

"I am from here," he says in his thick accent.

The girl smiles. "No you're not."

"Serious," Manuelo laughs.

Ryan feels a little awkward witnessing this flirting. Especially since the girls look thirteen.

* * *

"Check these fairies out," Doyle says giddily with a hand extended over the barrier ledge. Lennox walks out of DD's with the charm in a little bag, he and Rollo come over to the ledge to see what Doyle is pointing at. Lennox sees Ryan and that other kid downstairs chatting to some bitches that look like they haven't even gotten their first period.

"Ryan is such a piece of shit." Lennox gets an idea. He tucks the little bag from DD's in his pocket and swings his head around in search.

"What are you looking for?" Rollo asks.

"Ah-hah! Right here," Lennox says triumphantly as he heads over to a nearby decorative plant. Out of the plant's pot, he picks a smooth quarter-sized pebble and bounces it in his hand.

Doyle claps his hands in anticipation when he sees it.

* * *

"I have an early curfew," one of the young girls is shyly telling Manuelo.

Ryan keeps noticing the other cupcake giving him meaningful looks, and he wants to be a good wingman for Manuelo, but Ryan is nagged with a little worry that he could get in trouble just talking to this Lolita. *She is cute though.* He tries to appear very interested in a Leila poster dressing the music store they stand next to.

"We can pick you up later," Manuelo is telling his girl. "Have you not ever sneaked out?"

"I guess," the girl says.

"Yeah, we pick you up and you hang out with us. We have fun." Manuelo finishes his pitch with a cool puff from his cigarette.

"And do what?" the girl asks.

Ryan feels something whiz by his ear and hears a loud crack as it strikes the window behind him.

"What was that?" Manuelo asks.

Attracted by the noise, a security guard for the mall shouts at them from across the coffee stand, then starts over–a hostile look in his eyes.

Ryan sees Doyle, Rollo, and that asshole Lennox upstairs pointing and laughing. Lennox tosses a rock in his hand.

"What did you do to this window?" The security guard demands. He grabs Manuelo above the elbow and shakes him. "You can't smoke in here, kid! I want all of you little stains to come with me. I'm not going to let you disrespect this facility."

"We didn't do anything!" the lolita cries.

The security guy ignores her and pulls a walkie-talkie from his belt. "I need assistance by Music Unlimited."

The two young girls run away in complete dread.

"Hey, get back here!" The security is having a hard time holding Manuelo who is taking a cue from the girls.

Lennox and the others are having a hoot upstairs watching the whole thing. In a rage, Ryan snatches the walkie from the security's clutches and hurls it like a throwing star, it twirls end-over-end and strikes Lennox square in the side of his laughing face, knocking him over.

As Ryan rejoices, he is tackled from behind by the security guard. His head smacks hard on the edge of a bench and shoots shockwaves of pain through his face.

"You little shits!" The security wrestles Ryan to the ground and struggles to pin his arms down.

Manuelo punts the guard square in the testicles, but the security doesn't go down. It does lessen the pressure on Ryan, however, who spins around to knee the guy directly. The guard tries to keep fighting, but he has been weakened enough for Manuelo to help Ryan out of the hold. Ryan looks around and sees a dozen or so old people standing by, witnessing the entire affair, looking aghast but none apparently wanting to get involved.

"Ain't you dead *yet*!?" Ryan yells at them before he and Manuelo race off through the mall toward salvation.

"That was great!" Manuelo laughs as they speed away.

"You're a dirty fighter, Manuelo!" Ryan shoves a mannequin to the ground in his hasty getaway.

Without slowing down, Manuelo boots the mannequin head, sending it flying across the department store. "You too, my friend!"

"Did you see me get Lennox?"

"That was a good throw, man."

"We gotta go somewhere and celebrate!"

DINNER CONVERSATION

RYAN STUMBLES OUT OF MANUELO'S SUBARU AND collapses onto the lawn of Mallory's house.

"*Que te vaya bien*, Ryan," Manuelo salutes.

"*Adios*." Ryan waves farewell as Manuelo ramps the car onto the sidewalk, hitting over the garbage can before squealing away. Sooner than Ryan can knock on the door, Mallory answers.

"Hi..." Her smile vanishes as she sees Ryan's current state of disarray. She frowns at his puffy black and blue eye along with the scrape on his chin. She tsks at his rumpled clothes, too. "Did you get your ass kicked? Oh my gawd, have you been smoking?"

"Hello, Muffin," Ryan chimes.

"Try to keep it together," she orders, waving him in. "Dinner's almost ready."

Mallory's house is warm with family supper intimacy. Ryan catches the smell of sautéed chicken in the air and hears a small scrappy dog yap coming from somewhere in the house.

"My mom really wants to meet you," Mallory says. She leads Ryan into the living room where a balding man with a goatee is dressed like a real estate agent and watching a golf tournament on high volume. "This is my dad," she says to Ryan. "Dad, this is my friend Ryan."

The dad turns and looks Ryan over with a smile on his face, but distrust in his eyes.

"Nice to meet you," Ryan says.

"Yeah," says Mallory's dad. The two men shake hands. "A pleasure."

"Come meet my mom." Mallory leads Ryan into the dining room where an older version of Mallory is setting the dinner table. "Hi mom."

"Oh, Mallory," the mom says with a smile, "is this your little boyfriend? My, he's cute. If you cleaned him up a little, I mean."

"Likewise," Ryan says.

"This is Ryan," Mallory introduces.

"Here. You can sit here next to Mallory," the mother says. "You arrived right on time for dinner. Mallory, tell your father to come to the table." She gives Ryan a wide smile as she follows her daughter out of the room.

Ryan takes a seat where he was directed. He sits there, alone, listening to the cool jazz buzzing vaporously from the large stereo in the corner. *What is this music? I feel like my testicles are shriveling inside my body.* Mallory comes back in the room carrying a small dog; the same disgusting animal in the picture Ryan had laughed at in his previous visit. As soon as it sees Ryan, it starts yapping and wagging its hairless tail in a fit.

"Shut up, Precious!" Mallory scolds the dog. The repulsive animal is going wild in her arms, deciding between barking at Ryan and licking Mallory's face.

Ryan wouldn't touch the dog with the bottom of his boot, and his stomach does back flips at the sight of Mallory giggling with the dog licking her. *Ew, and on her mouth.* Mallory sets the dog down to take her seat. Ryan tries not to scream as the dog sniffs at his leg.

"Phil eagled on his last hole!" Mallory's dad is saying to the room as he comes in to take his seat. "Gosh, he's amazing. I could watch him all day. It's just the first round of the tournie, but my money is on him."

"Yeah?" Ryan fumbles for an appropriate response.

"You play golf?"

"I'm not really the team player type, sir." Ryan struggles momentarily to find some information about himself that he can offer. "I was in the automotive club a long time ago."

"Automotive?" the dad grumbles. "Did you check out my LS? What do you think of her? Baby's got three-hundred ninety horses, massaging seats, air ionizers. It's the total package. Confident, exhilarating, and powerful."

"Sounds...outstanding. I think it has three-eighty horses though."

"No. Three-hundred ninety," Mallory's dad says with authority.

"Um...okay."

"Do you want something to drink?" asks Mallory.

"Sure."

"Honey, get your friend a beer. And see if your mother needs any help while you're up. I don't know what's taking her so long."

"Alright, daddy." Mallory gets up from the table and exits the room.

Mallory's dad suddenly erupts in a titter of laughter. "You like Woody Allen?"

"I...uuuh..."

"Last night I was watching this movie he did recently, and it just had me rolling," Mallory's dad is telling Ryan merrily. "There was this line, and it was the way he said it, but I had to stop the movie, I was laughing too hard." The dad prepares himself to retell this anecdote by wetting his lips with a sip from his brew. "So Woody's at this arthouse full of snobs, right? And one of them asks him what his religion is. So he says–"

Mallory comes back into the room with Ryan's beer and a ceramic plate of lettuce that she sets on the table before taking her seat again.

"So he says to this really *snobby* character," Mallory's dad continues, his voice getting higher as the punchline nears bursting out of his mouth, "I used to be of the Jewish persuasion, but now I'm a narcissist!" The dad cackles loudly at the witty retelling.

"Isn't that funny?" Mallory asks him, a giant grin on her face.

Funny? About as funny as dipping a baby in honey and feeding it to ants. He attempts to delay a response by taking a drink from his beer. "Ah gawd!" he spits. "What the hell is this?" Ryan checks the label on the bottle. *Non-alcoholic!*

Mallory's mom comes in carrying an ornate bowl and wearing a grafted-on smile. "Isn't this nice?" she says airily, setting the bowl in the middle of the table and taking her seat. "Now everyone, help yourselves."

Despite her mother's words, Mallory dishes out some minced meat and vegetable medley to everyone, starting with her father. "What do you think of the serving ware?" Mallory asks Ryan. "My mom made them herself."

Ryan studies the malformed ceramic serving set and makes a sound, hoping it is accepted as a noise of fascination.

"It's just a hobby," the mom says with false modesty. "If you like any of them, I'll give you a fair price."

Ryan smiles crookedly in an attempt to hide the pain that must be showing in his eyes.

"This is how you eat lettuce wraps," Mallory's dad says to Ryan. "You take some of this lettuce, okay?" He takes a piece of lettuce and places it on his plate. "And then, you just put some of the meat inside," the dad continues to follow his words with a physical demonstration for Ryan's benefit, "and eat it–like a burrito! See?"

"Amazing," Ryan says through thin lips. "It looks tricky."

"You'll get a hold of it."

These people must think I have an extra chromosome. Ryan looks at Mallory's juicy lips, reminding himself of why he is there, and shrugs off the down-talk. He takes a bite of his food. "This is great," he says. "This is, um...this is exquisite."

"So, Ryan," the mom starts. "Do you go to school with Mallory?"

"Yes, ma'am."

"You're the first boy Mallory's introduced us to. This isn't your first boyfriend, is it sweetie?"

"We have a class together," Mallory snaps.

"Is this one of those bad boys?"

Ryan laughs at the accusation.

"Do you drink?" the mom asks Ryan pointedly. "You know we are recovering alcoholics? I can tell when someone drinks. It's an aura, like a stink."

"Leave him alone," Mallory says defensively.

Mallory's dad concentrates on his food, bobbing his head to the music from the stereo and completely ignoring the conversation.

"This is why I don't bring anyone over," Mallory whimpers.

"I don't know *anyone* you chum around with."

"Why do you think that is? You're so embarrassing."

"Yeah?" the mom says looking over at Ryan who is staring at the stereo.

"What kind of music *is* this?" Ryan asks. The music has been going off on a tangent that sounds like a three year old banging on a piano with no melody whatsoever along with a handicapped fingerless gorilla playing something like a pan-flute.

The dad perks up at Ryan's question. "It's a recorder! I play a little, but this guy here is a true master. See right here? Here comes a solo." The dad picks up his fork in both hands and closes his eyes, listening to the gobbledygook coming from the radio and munching on some food.

"Aw, dad!" Mallory cries.

"Shut up. Here it is." Mallory's dad uses his fork as if he was playing an air-recorder and vocalizes the notes, bobbing his head as he 'feels' the riff. "Do-dee-wo-wa-woo-WEEE–" At the high pitch, a half-eaten corn niblet shoots out of his mouth and into the bowl of chicken medley, "-Ya-do-Daaa-zee-ee-da!"

Ryan lets the lettuce wrap fall apart from his hand, back onto his plate, and wipes his tongue clean with the tablecloth. "I'm out," he says, standing up. Precious, the little rat dog, starts barking in a mad frenzy and follows Ryan to the door. "Get off me!" he hisses, kicking at the dog.

Mallory runs to stop Ryan from leaving. He is already half out the door, but turns to see what she has to say. She looks at him woefully, her mouth working to find the words.

"What a little prick," Mallory's mom says loudly in an obvious attempt to be heard from the other room.

Mallory just shakes her head in disappointment and defeat. Ryan reciprocates no emotion as he shuts the door on her.

37

"MOVE YOUR ASSES!" KERRY SCREAMS AS HE FLIES around the corner of a large brick building with a DVD player cradled in his arms. He simultaneously tries to keep the CDs and movies stacked on top from spinning off as he runs in a full high-kneed gallop down an Everdale inner-city street. Denise, her teeth set in effort, is keeping a long-legged pace right behind him with about twelve large gold necklaces swung around her left arm and two straight-hair wigs clutched in her right hand.

"Hey, wait up!" Arno calls ahead to Denise and Kerry racing in front of him. Arno is having a hard time keeping up with them in his stiff ambling stride while carrying his loot: a velvet three-piece suit on a hanger slung over his shoulder and a vat of ethnic hair gel under his arm. He is pouring sweat, eyes puffy and red, and he is lurching more than actually running.

A young man with dog-ear braids is screaming into his walkie-talkie phone like a murder is being committed, "Yo nigga! Yo, get up!" He is in pursuit of the teens, not too far behind Arno.

Dee-DEET "Whaaa?" comes the sleepy voice from the other end of the walkie-phone.

Arno's leg cramps up and he drops the hair gel on the pavement; it splatters everywhere in a shower of goop.

The man with braids is running in a full wind-sprint and yells into his phone, "Nigga, get up! Some crazy ass fuckas just jacked my shit!" He leaps over the sludgy spatter of gel in the sidewalk without missing a step.

Dee-DEET "Aw nigga. Quit playin'."

Kerry and Denise are far ahead, despite being winded and looking pale and sickly. Arno, on the other hand, has completely run out of steam and is hobbling on one leg. He tries to check the distance of his pursuer, but only trips himself up and stumbles to the ground in a crash. He lies there in a wheezing coughing spasm, struggling to breathe and claw his way toward freedom.

It only takes a second for the man in braids to catch up.

"I'M TELLING YOU, TURNING CITIES INTO LAKES!" A textbook Army recruiter, complete with shaved head and ironed khakis, is pitching the glories of military service to a small group including Ryan, Manuelo, and a couple others. The recruiter is taking a calculated informal stance at the table outside the Independence High cafetorium with one leg up on the seat of the table, but the group is treating him like a salesman that has wandered out of his mall kiosk and found his way to their break room.

Manuelo takes a drag from his cigarette. "That is bad ass, man."

"It's a great opportunity," the recruiter continues the spiel. "Pays for college. You learn discipline, too. As a warrior."

"Oh yeah?"

"It's very important these days." The recruiter tries to make eye contact with the full table. "It's a definite path to success. Let me ask you men something. And this is something that I want you to take home. Because this is what it's all about. A lot of people get comfortable and they forget how shitty the world is.

"They forget what makes this fine country so great, how *lucky* you all are, what countless men have given their lives to protect. When you guys are out playin' slap n' tickle with your friends, yeah it's funny so it's okay to laugh–you like that one right?–heavy pettin' with your sweet lil' Lizzy Anne, I want you to remember the heroes that have fought and bled for what so many today take for granted."

"What's the question?" Ryan takes the bait on purpose.

The recruiter smiles at Ryan and then becomes deadly serious. "The question is, men, have you got what it takes, the intestinal fortitude, have you got the *balls*, to become a heavily trained member of the greatest military force in the world, the US Army, and fight for freedom?"

"That sounds like a load of cow pucky," Ryan responds cynically.

"Excuse me?"

"I'd have to sign my life away to the *vultures*, and they don't give a damn about me. You just go out and die to make some sonofabitch richer. And if you survive, you wouldn't end up with any *skills* you could get rich with in civilian life. So what was the point? Discipline and freedom, my ass!"

The recruiter blinks at Ryan's offensive tirade and paints his smile back on. "Sounds like you're a little misinformed."

"If you could actually kill people, I'd do it for nothing," Ryan goes on. "I'd be the perfect soldier. I'd kill 'em all. Women, children... everybody."

"Well, son, the United States military doesn't take maniacs." The recruiter gives Ryan a condescending smile then cuts him out of the conversation completely. "So what are your plans after high school?" he asks Manuelo.

"I was going to go back to Mexico," Manuelo answers. He continues excitedly, "but if I can shoot the big guns, man? That would be ver' cool."

"Mexico? Are you a US citizen?"

Manuelo shakes his head.

"What about you?" the recruiter points to a third kid, a boy in a sports coat who appears very intoxicated.

"네 입에서 썩은 구토 냄새가 난다."

"God damn waste of time." The recruiter propels himself from the table in an angry sulk.

"Useless doodle dandy," Ryan says when the recruiter gets out of earshot.

"Soji, what did you say to him?" Manuelo asks the kid in the sportcoat. Soji just gazes at Manuelo with bloodshot eyes.

"Aw, Soji, you are fucked *up*, dude," Ryan says. Both Manuelo and Ryan share a laugh, and after a moment Soji joins in.

Mallory strolls by the table and very obviously pretends it doesn't exist. Ryan sees her and calls after her, but she continues walking without acknowledging him, so he gets up and chases after her. He stops her at the vending machine that sells only healthy snacks.

"Mal-lo-ry," Ryan pronounces.

Mallory tries to act surprised. "Oh, hello. *Ryan*."

"How's it going?"

"You working on your project?" she asks, referring to the table he was sitting at.

"No. I thought about the other day when I was at your house."

Mallory looks at him with a quirked eyebrow, waiting for him to get to the point.

"And you know," he continues, "I forgive you."

Mallory is blown away. "What?!"

"Hey, I wasn't trying to meet your mommy and daddy."

"Don't worry," Mallory whirls around to go, "I won't ask you over again."

"What, you got someone else?" Ryan calls after her. "Better not be cheating on me."

TRUTH

September 15, 1998
I was molested by a drunk old lady when I got to
work. I didn't even clock in yet. She took my
arm and told me to show her where the restroom
was so I walked her to it. She stopped me from
leaving and pinned me up against the wall. She
kept leaning in to kiss me and I was so shocked
I didn't know what to do and her mouth was
almost on mine and I was getting an erection so
I kissed her and she tasted like shit and her
dad interrupted us as he walked to the men's
room. I should have asked her for some money.

September 9, 1998
You can't force it.

August 30, 1998
Stuck inbetween desire to impress & desire for
personal satisfaction & relaxation I war with
myself and I know I'll lose. Lack of monetary
funds, decision is made without my opinion.
Worry and Fear threaten to incapacitate me.
Threaten to crush my confidence and strength. One
thing is certain. If I want to do what I want
to do, my wickedness must completely squash and
destroy utterly my feeling & compassionate self.
No good must ever be thought in my head. I must
be completely insensitive and creatively evil.

August 19, 1998
A people of materialism, unfocused on life
around them and distracted by shiny objects and
simple human affairs, are a people of the dead,
a civilization of comfortable corpses. Less than
slaves because a slave knows who he is. Those
blind to their slavery and numb to the passions
of liberty are empty vessels; living dead.

August 10, 1998
My life is filled with people I have never even
met. I have no jesus. I have jesuses. Imaginary
personal relationships with every public figure
every actor every voice every writer.

How many real people are in my life and how are
my relationships with them? How many people call
me in a day? How many friends do I have? How many
girls do I have? Where do I get my inspiration
for real life? What life is this that I have? I
need an adventure. I'm so old now. This society
has drained my youth just as I was afraid it
would. It's 18 years I'll never get back. 18
years and I've accomplished nothing and have had
minimal adventures I'm so uninteresting I just
can't stand it and for all my anger and tears the
only thing the only response from this life that
I have gotten since birth is FRUSTRATION. This
is my key feeling in Life. This does not lead
me to happiness. This is why money can lead to
happiness. It reduces the amount of things that
can frustrate me. This is the Truth.

August 5, 1998
I'm filled with a loneliness or rather, I'm
barren of companionship vacant but for a rotting
soul I don't belong on this world but I don't
belong anywhere else How pretentious am I? How
self-involved and arrogant? What am I going to
do with my life? Torn between wanting to be
great but being shit.

You will find nothing here but a void that
swallows all moral thought and laws.

UNDER THE COVER OF MOONLIGHT, RYAN, MANUELO, and Jeffrey are parked in silence a little way down the street from Mallory's home. Ryan refolds Jeffrey's journal and puts it in his pocket.

Manuelo sits in the passenger's seat of his Subaru with the window down, smoking casually. "You should forget this girl, man. She is not special."

"I just want to know," Ryan explains. He taps his gloved palm and naked fingers on the steering wheel impatiently before stilling himself and clenching his hand into a shaky fist.

After some more silence Manuelo says, "I do not think this thing helps," referring to Jeffrey in the back seat.

"What?" Ryan is questioning 'this thing'.

"Sure, if you do not like the pussy, I guess." Manuelo flicks his cigarette out the window. "But I do not think womans like this."

"Wait now," Ryan says quietly, pointing to a Pontiac GTO that pulls in front of Mallory's home. "Who the hell is this?" Ryan reads the license plate: BIG STF.

After a moment, Mallory gets out of the muscle car, waves goodbye to the driver, and saunters into her home.

"Screw this," Ryan fumes. "Let's get out of here."

Ryan, already ass-eyed drunk, spikes his soda with the flask of brandy and watches Manuelo break the triangle of billiard balls. The Fan Club UnLTD jukebox pumps a Leila track among their top twenty playlist, which is interrupted every so often by a helpful sales message. Jeffrey chills on a stool against the wall under his disguise of hat and sunglasses.

Manuelo, cigarette dangling from his mouth, takes another shot. "*¡Ay, no pinche puto pedo mames güey!*" Manuelo curses at his miss.

"Are you thirsty?" asks a voice over the sound system. "Our concessions carry over fifteen refreshing types of soda. Please party responsibly."

Ryan looks over the pool table for a shot. "I'm solids, right?"

"Ryan!" Kerry comes over to the pool table looking pasty, sweaty, and a little more than fidgety. His eyes land on Jeffrey and his brows shoot up his forehead in surprise. "Holy shit. You still got it?" he yells in disbelief.

"Jeez, Kerry," Ryan says, "you look like hell."

"What are you *doing*?" Kerry shrieks.

"Nobody cares. Manuelo doesn't care." Ryan takes his shot at the table, misses.

"Screw it," Manuelo agrees. "I do not care."

Kerry turns to Manuelo, looks him up and down, then back at Ryan. "I thought you got rid of it!"

Ryan realizes Kerry has the same wild look in his eyes that Denise had. "What's your story?" he asks Kerry.

Kerry moves in a jerk to face Jeffrey. He puts his nose right up to Jeffrey and examines him closely, peering under the sunglasses into the eye sockets as if the secret of life was inside. "You're not gonna beat me, you homosexual," Kerry promises through his teeth.

Manuelo misses the pocket. "Your go, Ryan."

"Food is energy," states a voice over the sound system. "Why not stop at the Nacho Bar for a spicy treat? Don't overeat!"

"So where is everyone else?" Ryan asks as he sights his shot.

Kerry is mesmerized by Jeffrey, shaking his head and grunting to questions Ryan can't hear.

"Hey!" Ryan demands attention. "Where's your girlfriend? Where's Arno?"

"Arno's dead, bro," sobs Kerry.

Ryan makes the shot in the corner pocket. "What?"

"Yeah, he died." Kerry now gives the news like giving the time. "Denise is at home. She thinks we got cursed. She won't leave her room."

"Wait. Arno's dead?" In a fit, Ryan slams his pool stick on the table, splitting it in two. *It's impossible.* "When did this happen?"

Kerry seems surprised at Ryan's display of emotion. "I've been looking for you, Ryan. I saw your car at school. What was left..."

"God dammit!" Ryan's skin prickles in shock. *Arno!* he screams in his mind. The scream multiplies exponentially in his head thousands of times, gushing into an atomic sun inside his skull until Ryan thinks his brain will explode out his ears. But the sound is only in his head. The screams are only in his soul.

"We got to take it back," Kerry implores, spittle flying from his mouth. "Put it back in the hole." He makes an attempt to grab Jeffrey, but is stopped by Ryan and what's left of his cue.

"Don't touch him," says Ryan.

"What the hell, scrote!" Kerry is hysterical, his mouth frothing. "We got to put him back!"

"Don't. Touch. Jeffrey." Ryan isn't playing games.

Kerry squeezes his fists, but seems to realize he is too weak to fight. "Listen, you have to believe me," Kerry whines. "We made a mistake, Ryan. Nothing's been right since we took it out of the ground."

"You're losing it."

"I thought you got rid of it!" Kerry seethes, trembling in a helpless fury, his eyes rolling in their sockets. Ryan returns to his pool game, using Manuelo's cue. "You'll see," Kerry warns. "You're going to regret it. You'll see!" Kerry runs away screaming.

"That guy is *loco*," Manuelo says.

Ryan wonders if there might be something to Kerry's story. He analyzes Jeffrey thoughtfully. Jeffrey remains on the stool with a huge grin on his face.

AMERICAN NIGHTMARE

41

ALABASTER GARGOYLES LEER AT RYAN ENTERING through the rusted cemetery gates. He takes his steps carefully as the burial grounds are blanketed in a gloomy fog. Delicate harp music hangs in the air, reverberating through the deep mist, .

From atop a gravestone, a colossal demonic vulture feasts on the guts of Libby, splayed out and disemboweled. Libby's plastinated face grins widely as the carrion feeder pecks at its scarlet flesh; the mascot's meaty insides squirming with maggots. The sinister bird cocks its featherless head to watch Ryan with beady yellow eyes, its beak dripping in the dark blood.

Ryan backs away from the bird, choking on his heart as it spreads its massive black wings and hisses at him. With speed Ryan didn't think was possible from a creature so large, the hell vulture takes to flight and swoops at his head. Ryan drops to the ground, barely managing to avoid the monstrous scavenger tearing at him with its pointed beak and claws. He rolls and spins to ready himself against another pass.

The misty air flashes and cracks, revealing Jeffrey The Corpse sitting high on top of a purple tombstone like a mountainous throne, cloaked in the American flag and strumming a harp made of an antelope skull. Ryan floats toward Jeffrey unwillingly, as if Jeffrey can summon all things in his land of the dead and home of the grave.

Ryan cranes his neck to look up at the grinning skull of Jeffrey who towers above him, now a hundred feet tall in the spacious sapphire sky. He finds his voice to ask, "Are you mad at me?"

From deep within Jeffrey's cavernous eye sockets comes a gleaming like twilight. Lightning flares red like a rocket through the cemetery, casting horrific shadows across Jeffrey's cadaverous visage and adding flesh to his decayed form, as if he has recomposed for a few years.

In a voice like a distant bonfire of burning kittens, a bonfire that echoes in a whisper through the cemetery, from everywhere, Jeffrey chants dolorously along to his morbid harp song:

Now we battle, till death's rattle,
The Rebel name carries no shame.
Strike with wrath and save! Conquer the path unpaved!
Don't Forsake! Freedom and Life!
Today Awake! Freedom or Death!

A figure claws its way out of the earth, and Ryan comes face to face with himself, or a darker, distorted version of himself. The Distorted Ryan beholds Jeffrey through vulture's eyes and hisses in triumph, "I'm free!"

"Who are you?" Ryan demands fearfully.

The Dark Ryan turns his yellow eyes on Ryan in much of the same manner the hell vulture had looked at him. "I'm you," he seethes, thunder booming.

"Liar!" Ryan yells at the top of his lungs, "I am an eagle!" But his cry is suffocated in the sound deadening fog.

Ryan's reflection cackles villainously, his voice amplified across the mist, strong enough to weigh down on Ryan like a giant hand. "You were *never* an *eagle*."

In the havoc of terror, Ryan flees, and the malevolent laughter chases him. He comes to a 'T' in the road and faces a 'One Way' sign that points in both directions. To the right is a small path that leads to a shore of dark waters and in the far distance–like morning's first beam–is a wavering pinprick of light. To the left is a well-lit people mover like Ryan has seen inside airports.

The ominous laughter hunting him explodes like a bomb in the air, now so close he can almost feel its heat on his neck. In the near distance, Ryan spots Kerry riding the people-moving road. He makes a quick decision and hops on the human conveyer-belt toward his friend, rapidly adding distance between himself and the crossroads with giant strides.

"Kerry!" he calls, but Kerry doesn't turn around. Ryan looks ahead farther up the people mover and is stunned by the otherworldly spectacle of a giant red, white, and blue stage surrounded by fire that bridges the moving path. An eyeless Leila Caverns performs under its limelight like a ghastly vision of alluring depravity; her lithe sensuality belying her soulless decadence. She tempts Ryan and Kerry to approach her fiery stage whilst displaying her provocative dance choreography, cooing her hit song like a macabre lullaby:

> *O baleful rotted bones,*
> *For soul's undead dance,*
> *Four shed breath for atone,*
> *All gain death a chance!*

"Kerry?" Ryan grabs Kerry's shoulder to get his attention. "Where does this go?"

"Gobble-gobble," Kerry says, looking at Ryan with a blank stare.

"Bitch!" Ryan's irritation at his friend quickly turns to horror as he sees that just underneath Leila's pyrotechnic altar, the people mover drops off into a giant gorge. "Kerry, we have to go back!" He grabs Kerry by the arm and tries to pull him in the opposite direction the road is moving, but the road speeds up. Ryan walks faster, but the road moves faster. He lets go of Kerry and runs, but the human-conveyer matches his speed. Kerry goes under Leila's stage and falls off the edge to his destruction. Running and running, Ryan is pulled closer to the rift while the eyeless Leila flows seductively through her oversexed patriotic number.

Ryan is dragged under her stage and plunges into the chasm, landing in an open grave, but not an empty one: he is accompanied by the gruesome corpse of Arno. The Ryan with vulture's eyes, dressed like a Confederate Uncle Sam, pitches dirt in the grave, hitting Ryan in the face with a splatter of clods.

"Wait!" coughs Ryan. "I'm not dead!"

The distorted Ryan just laughs in the peeling thunder, tosses in more dirt and chides, "You think anyone's going to miss you?"

Ryan's screams are swallowed into dreadful silence by the earth that consumes him under everlasting oblivion.

42

AT SUNRISE RYAN WAKES UP WITH HIS FACE IN THE steering wheel of Manuelo's car and he opens his eyes to the noxious sight of Jeffrey propped in the passenger seat. He rubs the sleep from his eyes with a groan and sees Manuelo curled up in the tiny back seat. They are parked in some neighborhood Ryan doesn't immediately recognize. He has no memory of how he ended up at this moment, but with his pounding headache and dragon breath, he can guess it involved a lot of brandy. Tendrils of recollection about a demon vulture and star-spangled corpse creep into Ryan's head with hazy recollection. He stares at Jeffrey for a length in silence as more cognizance returns.

"I thought I *knew* you," he accuses Jeffrey through his teeth.

"…"

"I don't think we can be friends anymore," Ryan continues, shaking his head. "You killed Arno, didn't you? You killed The Defiler! That's *not* okay."

"…"

"I think you should get out of the car." Ryan starts up the sporty Subaru. "Let's not make this weird, okay?"

" . . ."

Ryan bites his lip in a sneer then leans over and angrily opens the passenger door. "Get out of the car, murderer!" Ryan screams as he pushes Jeffrey out of the car and speeds away, leaving him in a cloud of dust. Manuelo peeks up from the back seat and looks around in a daze before flopping back down.

RYAN PACES IN THE DESERT GARDEN OUTSIDE ETHICS class. He sniffs at his wrinkled clothes he had slept in–they reek of cigarettes–and he thoughtlessly touches the somewhat swollen area around his left eye. He noticed earlier that the color has changed from black to a brown tinge.

He can see Mallory and Lennox through the classroom window, already giving their oral presentation in the front.

* * *

Mallory is dressed in her recitation outfit of business casual as she stands at the podium in front of her classmates. In a confident voice she reads aloud, "Morals and values help us make decisions to," she gestures for Lennox to switch the slide to the bullet points as she reads from her note cards, "not have sex before marriage. Not drink until twenty-one. And to not cheat or steal."

Lennox wears business casual also, but his professional guise is slightly spoiled with the dark bruise on his cheek. He waves some papers in the air saying to the class, "My mother works for Super Copy Unlimited and, uh, she gave me this handout here." He sets the papers on Charles' desk, who looks at the text-only document with disinterest. Lennox continues, "This handout which shows her company's corporate values."

"Just look it over and pass it around," Mallory instructs Charles as she puts a graphic up that has the corporate values numbered.

"Value one." Lennox proceeds to read off the screen, "Teamwork. We learn from each other and share our skills and resources across organizational boundaries for our customers' benefit and our own. It is the essence of our ability to succeed as a trusted preferred supplier of solutions to our customers. Our overriding loyalty is to the good of the organization as a whole."

* * *

"What is happening in there?" Manuelo asks Ryan in a groan.

"That must have been *some* shit," Ryan laughs.

"Food here upsets my stomach." Manuelo winces and clutches his abdomen.

"Let's go in."

"It looks like there is a talk happening," Manuelo observes.

Ryan barges into the class anyway and Manuelo has no choice but to follow the lead.

"Team members should always have their smiles on," Lennox is saying as Ryan and Manuelo take their seats.

The teacher pauses the speech with a raised hand at Lennox. "You two are late," the teacher says in a grievous tone. "I'm going to have to mark you for interrupting the presentation." The teacher gives a nod for Lennox to carry on.

"Value three." Lennox names off the last on the list. "Diversity. We respect every individual of the team. The team draws strength from equal opportunity and diversity, at the same time supporting personal growth and development. We value and we all benefit from the entrepreneurial spirit of each individual."

"In having a good value system it will help all of us become good adults," Mallory presents. She delivers the last part like a lashing, with her eyes on Ryan. "And when you have no morals or values you just remain an immature child. You'll think you're Peter Pan and you'll never grow up, and *no one* will love you."

The two return to their seats while the class gives the obligatory applause, but Ryan can't keep his comments to himself. "That was complete bunk!" he says.

"Oh really, Mister Ryan? You think you can do better?" The teacher sounds doubtful.

"Absolutely," Ryan says.

"Then you can go next."

Ryan turns to Manuelo and asks, "What's it on?" Manuelo shows him the handout entitled: 'What is the importance of values and ethics in today's world?'. Ryan laughs. "Splendid."

"Alright then. Let's hear it," says the teacher sibilantly.

Ryan and Manuelo get up in front of the class.

"I am not okay about this," Manuelo whispers to Ryan.

"Just write on the board," Ryan instructs.

Manuelo spreads his hands in acquiescence and finds a dry-erase marker while Ryan takes a lazy stance at the podium.

"Morals, values, and ethics," Ryan starts. "These are some things that a few of you, I'm sure, know *nothing* about."

Manuelo starts writing 'Morals Values and Ethics' on the board, but misspells them in weird ways. Ryan uses his eyes to focus his speech on Mallory, Lennox, and the teacher.

"I'm glad I'm up here," he proceeds. "See, some of you out there think that even though you are a dirty skank, or an a-hole, or some elegant pervert, you can appear to be righteous. As if you knew a thing about morals. But basically, you're just hypocrites! All you slaves are kept from succeeding, due to concepts like morals, when, today's society is an amoral system. A capitalistic society where selling your soul is applauded. None of you really believe in individual rights or *freedom* anymore. You only believe in buying junk and being pat on the back for conforming to what everyone calls ethics. Ethics are why Corporations Unlimited owns ninety percent of this country! *Ethics* are what keeps poor people enslaved and what stops them from killing the rich."

"I think you are going off the topic," the teacher interrupts.

"How so?" Ryan asks.

"The assignment was why we need these institutions. Not on how to be an extremist."

"Okay, okay." Ryan looks at his feet as he thinks at the podium for a moment. "I got it." He raises his head and clears his throat. "In the vulture's nest lies the corpse of freedom. Okay? The corpse that has been devoured by the scumbags that live off of the masses. The vultures. Let's just say that today's values, ethics and morals are like the vulture's vomit. Vomit that keeps all you turkeys in line, you know, as a functioning clog in the machine.

"This regurgitated freedom no longer contains true integrity or heart. What you're left with is just a bunch of rules based on lies that bring no honor or glory or valuable existence! And there is always more vomit piling on top of old. More rules. A never-ending spew. The more freedom they eat, the more they puke on us all."

Ryan studies the reaction–or lack thereof–from his audience. "In closing I'd like to say that each of you has the ability to change the world. As long as you be good, obey the law, and have the most money." Ryan ends his sarcasm with a direct remark to Mallory. "So you might as well be honest about just doing whatever you want. You're going to do it anyway."

"I think that's enough," the teacher says. "You can stop now."

"Bravo, jackass," Lennox mocks.

"Encore!" applauds Charles.

"You know, I spoke to Mr. Jenkins this morning," the teacher says. "He's never heard of you, Ryan."

"Yeah, you're right," he admits.

The teacher is dumbfounded. "What are you doing?"

"Let's say I *was* in this class. What grade would I have gotten?"

"An *F*."

"What did I get?" Manuelo asks.

"You got a C."

"That's bullshit!" Ryan bursts in outrage.

"I think you'd better leave, mister." The teacher crosses his arms for punctuation.

"Sit on it." Ryan kicks the door open on his way out.

"DID YOU GET THE SURVEILLANCE VIDEO FROM SUPER Mart?" McCready asks Sapps.

Sapps playfully tosses a videotape from his desk over to McCready at the TV. "It should be cued up."

McCready pops the tape into the VCR and hits play. A four-way split screen of surveillance footage shows up on the TV monitor and McCready takes a step back for a better view. "Alright, let's take a gander."

Sapps says after a moment, "That's them right there."

"These are the suspects?" McCready laughs. "They all went in together on a little shopping spree, huh? Needed the new Chizzy CD I bet."

"They bought a comforter–"

"I guess they needed that."

"–and other junk."

"If they bought a bunch of *food*, I might feel sorry for them. It's easy to hate criminals when they steal for no good reason."

"Excuse me, sirs." It's Reeves. "I have someone here I think you should speak to." Reeves points to a nerdy teenager standing behind him.

"Alright Reeves. Thank you," Sapps dismisses him.

McCready stops the VCR. "What's up kid?"

The kid steps forward. "Well, I just came in to report a robbery, at my work, um, officer."

"Detective, kid. I'm a detective," McCready corrects. "What is it?"

"Yeah, well, my name's Kevin," Kevin says in a disrespectful tone. "Uh, I was working, and this carload of wannabes stole their food, and corporate wanted me to come down and make a report since I was the eye witness. I brought the receipt."

"So? Why did Reeves bring you to *us?*" McCready asks.

"I'm not sure…I just mentioned that they had a zombie with them, or what I thought was a zombie or something, but it looked real–bugs on it–and I could just tell it was real and not some paper-machè dummy like in theater–"

"What are you talkin' about?" Sapps cuts in. He looks how McCready feels: like he just got kicked in the gut.

Kevin goes on with his report, indifferent to the policemen's sudden interest. "These guys, a whole car of them, I think four, probably my age. Uh, brown hoopty, and they were covered in dirt. One was wearing a ski mask, so I probably couldn't ID him, and one, they called him Kerry, hit me. So I guess they could also be charged with assault."

"You say that you saw a group of kids with a zombie? You think it was probably a corpse?" McCready asks.

"Well yeah, that's pretty much the same thing. A corpse."

"When was this?" Sapps asks.

Kevin looks to the sky in remembrance. "It was the early hours of the sixth."

"And you're just *now* coming in?" McCready is flabbergasted.

"I was working."

"Doing what?"

"I am Team Leader at Quickie Food," Kevin says defensively.

McCready plows ahead. "A group of kids? Are you sure that there wasn't a middle-aged man with them?"

"I really don't think so. I'm sure it was a corpse," Kevin says in confusion.

"He said one was wearin' a mask," Sapps says optimistically to McCready and then asks Kevin, "Do you think that the one wearin' the mask could have been an older man, probably fifty?"

Kevin scratches his head. "I doubt it."

"Why?"

"He didn't sound old. He sounded young. Like a teenager."

McCready rubs his hands through his hair. He can feel his blood pressure rising and he turns to Sapps in a barely restrained meltdown. "Get that waste Fancy out of holding and out of this fucking station, now!"

45

RYAN HAS THE RADIO ON SOMETHING UP-BEAT AS HE drives Manuelo's SVX down an Everdale neighborhood with Manuelo in the passenger seat and two foreign exchange students, Nardia and Veronica, in the back. He makes eye contact with caterpillar-browed Nardia through the rearview and asks, "How do you girls like those beers?"

"Oh yes," Nardia says enthusiastically, "I very much like beer." She takes a chug from her bottle to prove it and wipes some dribble off her chin.

"Veronica?" Manuelo flicks his cigarette out the window and summons the girl who has on a traditional headdress worn by Arab and Muslim women. "What street is the party on?"

Veronica sticks her hijab-draped head up to the front and says with a thick accent, "It's just up here, where all the cars are."

Manuelo leans over to confide in Ryan. "We just need a place to sex these *putas.*"

"That sounds like a good plan," Ryan laughs. "You know these aren't even American girls?"

"What do you mean?"

"Uh...nothing." Ryan has a bit of luck when he finds a parking spot close to what appears to be the epicenter of the party surrounded by a crowd of vehicles. The crew make their way to the yard of the party house after finishing off their open beverages.

"They got a live band here?" Ryan asks.

"Maybe."

At the porch stoop, two large guys in trench coats lurk under a dim light, thumb-wrestling. Manuelo goes straight for the door, but he is pushed back by one of the toughs.

"Hey, man!" Manuelo exclaims in surprise.

One of the trench coat guys frowns over the four teens one-by-one. "This is a private party," he snarls.

"We got invited," Ryan says quickly.

"The hell you did," bites the other trench coat guy.

A skuzzy-looking longhair dude that smells like a dumpster, slides his way past Ryan and crew and into the party without any question. Ryan swings his head around to see if he is on a hidden camera show.

Manuelo's voice hardens. "What is the problem, man?"

"This isn't your kind of party," the first door guy says with a back-handed chopping motion. "So kick rocks."

"Is Lou in there?" Ryan asks. "Go find Lou. He'll vouch for us."

The door to the party flies open and out runs a pasty-skinned and frizzle-haired Denise, shoving her way through the two door guys. Ryan recognizes her before she recognizes him and tries not to be noticed, but fails. In a blind reaction, Denise flings herself at him like a bloodthirsty vampire and tries to scratch his face off.

"You son of a bitch!" she wails, her eyes raging with hatred. "It's all your fault!"

"Whoa!" Ryan defends her strikes effortlessly. "Calm yourself."

Again the door swings open, this time it's Kerry—who also looks worse for wear—getting thrown out by the back of his neck.

"Don't let this goatse bitch back inside," orders the guy throwing Kerry out. "And that goes double for his whore, too!"

The two door guys in trench coats grab Kerry and Denise and struggle to pull them off of the property.

"Kerry, hey," Ryan calls after them, "what's going on in there?"

Kerry writhes in the large doorman's grasp, his face explodes in anger at seeing Ryan. "You cursed us," he spits as he's dragged away. "You're out of the posse!"

"Kerry!" Ryan yells back at them as they are physically removed from the premises. "Are there any chicks inside?"

Manuelo grabs Ryan by the shoulder. "Come on, let us get amazing."

"Before they get back," Nardia adds in reference to the doormen.

Ryan leads the group unopposed through the red door of the house and into the party.

46

"HEY *CHICAS*, LET ME GIVE YOU THE TOUR." MANUELO herds Veronica and Nardia through the crowd of loud partiers with a hand at their waists. They pass the living room where some people are playing darts and watching some hardcore pornography.

Through the sliding patio doors that lead to the backyard, Ryan can see a heavy metal band performing; their music vibrating the entire house like a jet engine. He laughs when he spots a kid wearing a sportcoat going berserk, slam dancing amid a cluster of teens. "Manuelo!" Ryan yells above the noise. "Check out Soji!"

"Serious!" Manuelo laughs.

"You know that guy?" Veronica asks.

"He's always the life of the party," Ryan tells her. "He's a genius."

"Grab some drinks and come up," Manuelo tells Ryan when they reach the foot of the staircase.

Ryan nods. "Alright. Warm 'em up for me."

"*Por supuesto, cochino.*" Manuelo smacks the girls on their butts and chases them up the stairs.

Ryan battles through the crowded house toward where he imagines the kitchen to be. *This place is like a maze!* He comes across a room where a group is having a video game tournament.

"Open the door, Ryan," someone says from the game room.

Ryan looks around, confused for a second, before he realizes that someone was talking to a different kid in that room, evidently also named Ryan. The other Ryan–who looks like he is still in junior high–groans as he puts his game on pause, gets up from his crouch in front of the TV, and walks over to the closet door and pulls it wide open. Inside the closet are a couple of teens, both of their pants down.

"You lonely perv-o!" the girl in the closet screams as she grabs the door and slams it shut. The gamers burst out in raucous laughter.

So far, Ryan really likes this party's style. When he finally gets to the kitchen, he vaguely notices a group of people gathered around a table. He avoids the keg line and grabs a bottle of whiskey off the refrigerator. When he turns to head upstairs, something in the group catches his eye.

Sitting at the card table, with a frosty beverage in front of him, is the grinning corpse, Jeffrey. It appears that Jeffrey and four others are playing a beer game. It's 'Asshole' and Jeffrey has an empty twelve pack on his head to represent that he's 'it'.

"Left drinks!" crows one of the players at the table, which sets off a little fanfare.

Ryan stalks over to the table. "Are you kidding me?" he questions Jeffrey indignantly. "What the hell are you doing here? You're coming with me!" Ryan makes an attempt to grab Jeffrey, but is stopped with a hand on his wrist.

"Back up, Ryan." Rollo squeezes Ryan's wrist before throwing it back at him. He and Doyle are the other players at the table.

"Necrophuker," Doyle curses at Ryan, his eyes flashing.

* * *

The skeletal man is on patrol, riding on his steel steed that must have been forged in hellfire, cutting through the streets of Everdale with razorblade precision. From behind his dark sunglasses, his haunting eyes scour the roadside.

His brow quirks when he comes to one particularly busy street. He slows down to inspect the vehicles parked along the lane. It doesn't take him long to spot Manuelo's blue Subaru. When he does, the skin stretched along his face wrinkles into a devilish grin that darkness itself seems to exude from.

* * *

Ryan is caught in a stare down with the table of 'Asshole' players, his teeth clamped in determination. "You're a ghoulie," he tells Rollo, meeting his gaze firmly.

"If you want to join the game, pull up a chair," says the player Ryan doesn't know.

"He's not joining the game," Rollo says matter-o-factly.

"I don't want to join the game!" Ryan snaps. "I'm going to take my corpse and leave."

"You're not touching Eddie, Ryan." Doyle's words drip with malice.

Manuelo runs in the kitchen and spots Ryan. "Come on man! The girls are making out! Serious!"

Ryan rounds on Manuelo and points an accusatory finger at Jeffrey. "Why is *he* here, Manuelo?"

"Who?" Manuelo blinks in confusion.

"You're coming with me you son of a bitch!" Ryan lunges across the table and grabs Jeffrey by the shoulders, but Rollo has his grip on Jeffrey as well. "Stop it!" Ryan yells, but Rollo won't give up. "You're hurting him!"

Rollo tears at Jeffrey just as Ryan makes a final attempt at yanking him free. Ryan falls to the ground as he wins the tug-of-war, but bounces back to his feet, holding Jeffrey like a prize. "We're out of here."

But Rollo holds a prize of his own: Jeffrey's arm that has detached at the elbow. Rollo looks at the limb in his grasp, turns it around and waves the corpse-hand at Ryan. "See ya, dork."

The whole table burts out laughing, but Ryan's blood boils. "That's not yours!"

Rollo scratches his butt with Jeffrey's hand. "Gee, you're really falling to pieces."

"Hack!" Ryan snatches at a nearby beverage and hurls it at Rollo, but Rollo uses the arm to block.

Doyle jumps out of his chair and kicks Ryan in the leg. Ryan tries to fight Doyle off, but he is tackled to the ground by Rollo while the other teens around the table shout and cheer. Manuelo quickly gets over being stunned, and pounces into the fray, jumping on Doyle's back and delivering a rake to the eyes.

* * *

The man with the mangled left ear stands like gloom incarnate at the door of the party, but the two large guys in trench coats are back at their stations and bar his way.

"Get lost, old fart," one of them says boldly. "No narcs allowed."

The man in black makes no expression, his face wooden. He slowly raises his bony right hand in front of his face, fingers outstretched. The black sleeve of his jacket drops to reveal the green, blue, and yellow tattoos that wrap around his forearm in soft designs and travel up his elbow like nymphs playing in watery vines. His face follows his hand as he lifts it towards the sky, wiggling his fingers as if casting a spell. The doorman in front of him watches the raised hand curiously.

In shocking speed, the skeletal man slaps the door guy hard across the face with the back of his open hand, knocking the large doorman off his feet to tumble from the stoop.

"Kenny!" the remaining door guy yells after his fallen friend.

The skeletal man moves like a striking viper to grab the second doorman by the throat and choke him to his knees. He pulls his sidearm with his left hand that is covered in sharp tattoo designs colored red, orange, purple, like screaming souls drowning in flowing blood and burning in razor fire, and presses the barrel of the Double Eagle to the kneeling man's forehead. "Can't an old man party?"

The man on his knees shudders with complete terror at the weapon pointed at his brains, as if death were the saddest thing that could happen to him.

* * *

Doyle is on the ground with his hands over his eyes, writhing in pain. Both Ryan and Manuelo are on top of Rollo, pummeling him.

"Get the car!" Ryan yells. Manuelo jumps up and runs out of the kitchen area.

Ryan takes a moment to catch his breath and find Jeffrey's arm, as both Rollo and Doyle seem to have been defeated. The kids from the card table are staring at him like he is some rabid animal.

"You should probably get out of here," says the teen that had offered a seat to Ryan.

Ryan clubs Doyle in the face with Jeffrey's arm and Doyle starts crying. He picks up Jeffrey at the same instant Mallory and Lennox walk into the room. Ryan sees that they are holding hands and on Mallory's wrist is the same charm he saw Lennox buy at the mall.

"You're with the wrong guy," he tells her.

Mallory stands in bewildered silence, her face an image of disgust. Lacking an appropriate verbal response, she just shakes her head at him.

"It looks like you need an ass kicking," Lennox tells Ryan.

* * *

The grim man searches through the rooms of rowdy teens with the dark determination of a hungry wolf. He clenches the .45 caliber double-action pistol in his left hand as he briskly scans the young drunk faces in the billiard room. With a growl, he spins out into the hallway and comes across a locked door. He steps back, takes aim, and blows the handle apart with a boom. He kicks it open to discover two young girls–one wearing a scarf on her head–deeply enjoying each other's company.

* * *

Ryan cradles Jeffrey closer, and points at Lennox with Jeffrey's arm. "Get out of my way, Lennox."

Lennox pushes Mallory back gently and puts up his fists.

"You should be ashamed," Mallory spits at Ryan.

All of a sudden, Doyle grabs Ryan at the knees, tripping him, and screams, "Take the body! Quick, take it!"

Lennox snatches up Jeffrey and kicks Ryan. "Fuck you, fucker! Come and get it!" Lennox knocks Mallory out of the way as he runs from the room with Jeffrey over his shoulder.

"You asshole!" Mallory yells after him.

Ryan delivers an elbow to Doyle and goes after Lennox. With Jeffrey's severed limb, he swats party people who stand in the way of his chase. As he rushes out of the front door, Manuelo pulls up in his Subaru and opens the passenger door for Ryan. Ryan swings his head around, but there is no sign of Lennox or Jeffrey. "Where did they go?"

"I did not see anyone," says Manuelo.

Ryan jumps into the car. "Lennox took Jeffrey! We got to get him!"

A police cruiser pulls up in front of the Subaru, flashing its red and blue lights, and an Adonis-type officer steps out. "Turn off your car!"

"What do we do?" Manuelo asks Ryan.

"Take the keys out of the ignition and place them on the dash!" orders the cop.

Ryan spots a man bursting through the doorway like an enraged phantom. "Let's go!" he screams as the man aims the pistol at him.

The officer becomes aware of the gun-wielding man in the doorway and grabs at his sidearm, shielding himself behind his cruiser. "Put it down!" he orders as he points his own weapon at the man cloaked in black.

The man who resembles a skeleton calmly turns his attention to the officer, breathing in through his teeth, he raises his chin at the policeman.

"Put the gun d–!" A giant white truck blasts the officer from behind, throwing him into the air like a bad TV show stunt dummy, his head landing with a sickening crack on the pavement.

Ryan and Manuelo stare in shock at the motionless body in uniform until a hole is blown in Manuelo's window from the furious man on the house stoop.

"Follow that truck!" Ryan yells to Manuelo.

Manuelo shifts into reverse and slams on the pedal; a few shots are fired at the Subaru as they tear after Lennox. Manuelo watches through the mirrors, heading to a four-way stop.

"Watch out!" Ryan screams.

Manuelo expertly pulls the handbrake, jams the steering wheel, and skids two-hundred-seventy degrees around a coupe of ghost-faced passengers to launch the Subaru head-on toward the fleeing white Chevy.

"I can not see him!" Manuelo wails. "Where did he go?"

"He went this way, right?" Two heartbeats later, Ryan sees the pitchfork-like front end of the nightmare Buick roaring down the road after them in intense pursuit. "Holy shit!"

"Who is that, man?" Manuelo has noticed the Buick, too. Through the Subaru's side-mirror, Manuelo sees the man peek out of the Riviera's window brandishing a shotgun. "*¡Hijo de la puta madre!*"

Manuelo takes evasive action, weaving perilously between traffic, barely managing to avert a colossal accident.

"He's gaining on us!" Ryan shrieks.

The Subaru screeches around a tight corner, hitting much of the curb, but the Riviera is still tailing and rapidly catching up.

"You're gonna kill us!" cries Ryan as Manuelo veers into oncoming traffic. At breakneck speed, Manuelo sideswipes a mini-van, sending it skidding into the chasing Buick's path, forcing their pursuer hit the brakes to avoid collision.

"There's Lennox!" Ryan points to the large white truck vanishing around a corner into a neighborhood community.

Manuleo bounces across several lanes of traffic as he cuts after it.

* * *

"Those licks want to play, huh?" Lennox screams at his dead passenger as he sees the blue car follow him into Blanquito Village. "I ain't fuckin' playin'!" He hits his wiper fluid to clean off some sort of smear on the windshield.

Without responding, the corpse jostles in its seatbelt as Lennox hits the speed-humps at high velocity.

* * *

"Why are you slowing?"

"There is a bump in the road," answers Manuelo.

"You can take it!" Ryan encourages, keeping his eyes in a constant volley between looking ahead for Lennox and looking behind for the devil car, who he hasn't seen enter the neighborhood. "Come on!"

Manuelo hits the next hump fast, sending Ryan's head to crack into the ceiling and the car to groan and creak painfully, but Manuelo continues to speed through the winding residential road.

After a bend, they once again lose sight of the white truck.

"This place is another rattrap."

"Where is he?" asks Manuelo.

"Right here!"

The tires of the Subaru scream with Manuelo's furious engineering, stopping the car to face the entrance of a short dead-end street that ends in a blockade. The street is lined with several homes, but there is no white Chevy truck in sight.

"Does he live here?" Manuelo wonders.

Ryan shakes his head. "Let's check down there," he says, using Jeffrey's arm to point out a back alley that runs behind all of the houses.

As Manuelo creeps the car toward the entrance, a GTO parked along the street catches Ryan's eye. A guy with slicked-back hair that Ryan feels he should recognize sits on the hood chatting to some chick, both trying to see into the Subaru.

"Okay, man," Manuelo gestures ahead of them down the alley, "we found him. Now what?"

Lennox must have backed in, because the giant Chevy is facing them from the far end of the tight backway.

"We got him," says Ryan. "Let's get–" The top light-rack on the Chevy turns on, flooding the Subaru with light and blinding Ryan and Manuelo. "What the hell is this?"

The Chevy starts to roll toward them slowly, then its horn blares through the night like a howling gorilla.

"Maybe we should get out of here," Ryan says quietly to Manuelo.

Spitting gravel into the air, the monstrous truck rears with torque, still piercing the air with its wailing horn, to charge directly at the sporty SVX.

"We're about to become roadkill!"

Manuelo jams the car into reverse and hits the gas, but the Chevy has gained speed, rushing at them faster than they can get away.

* * *

Lennox screams in unison with the horn of his truck, caught up in the frenzy of destroying his enemy, juiced with the high-pitched fervor of playing with disaster, inches away from crushing the little blue Subaru.

The next moments are a blur of events as inexplicably, the blue car reaches the alleyway exit and veers sharply, but not in time to avoid Lennox's charge completely. Weightlessness briefly overtakes Lennox as he sails through the air, just before the truck lands, crashing sideways into a parked mobile home.

* * *

"Are you guys hurt?"

Ryan and Manuelo gingerly get out of the car, and glance at the demolished front-end of the Subaru; the only part that the Chevy had driven over since they had reached the alley's entrance in time to avoid it going directly over them. They give each other a look that shows they are thinking the same thing: they got lucky.

"Are you guys hurt?" the guy with slicked hair asks them again, his one earring bouncing erratically. "We saw the whole thing. I'll testify to it."

"Oh my god," Ryan mutters as he sees the wreck of Lennox's Chevy turned on its side among the disastrous remnants of a mobile home.

"Katie," the guy yells to the girl still standing by the GTO, "call an ambulance!" The girl sprints into the house.

"What are you doing?" Manuelo calls after Ryan, who is jogging over to the critical accident.

"I've got to help him!" Ryan pushes debris and wreckage out of his way as he climbs on top of the truck to be able to reach into the driver's side window. "Are you okay?"

Lennox groans softly, blood gushing from his face in a crimson mask.

"Say something!" Ryan screams. "I'm going to help you!"

"…Ryan?" Lennox mumbles.

Ryan braces himself then bends into the truck. "You're gonna make it! Just hold on."

"Your friend's a hero," slick-haired guy tells Manuelo with admiration.

Manuelo lights his cigarette and just watches as Ryan pulls Jeffrey out of the ruined truck.

"I got him!" Ryan cries with exultance.

"Maybe an ambulance is a little late," remarks the guy.

"You…piece," Lennox coughs in pain, "…of…shit…"

Manuelo reads the keychain hanging from the GTO's ignition, "Big…stuff?" then starts up the Pontiac and revs the engine.

"Hey!" The guy, presumably Big Stuff, starts toward his car in reactive shock. "What are you thinking?"

"Back off!" Ryan commands, waving the severed arm at the guy while hugging Jeffrey close. "My friend will kick your ass."

"Katie!" Big Stuff yells. "Call the cops!" He jumps halfway into the driver's window in an attempt to grab the keys out of the ignition, but Manuelo puts a lit cigarette in his eye, sending him to the asphalt screeching.

Ryan helps Jeffrey into the Pontiac's back seat. "Move over, Manuelo. It's my turn."

A shiver shoots through Ryan's being, harkening the arrival of the grim warrior riding upon his destruction-mobile. The Buick creeps like lurking necrosis and stops at the only exit to the dead-end road.

"He is a terminator!" Manuelo gasps in disbelief, eyes fixed on the abysmal vehicle that blocks their path.

"Get down!" Ryan directs. "I don't think he knows we're in here."

The GTO's door flies open and slick-haired Big Stuff, clutching his eye, hollers, "Out of my car! I'm gonna fuckin' annihilate you!"

Ryan crushes the gas pedal to the floorboard, the Pontiac does a wheel stand, burning the asphalt, and spins toward the blockade in the opposite direction of their hunter. Big Stuff is flung to the ground and has to roll out of the way to avoid being crushed by the Buick. The Riviera is right behind as the GTO smashes through the blockade and races onto a patch of untamed earth.

"Hold on!" Ryan hollers. "We're coming to a service road!"

"He is right behind us, man!" Manuelo informs as they skid onto the smoother service road and pick up speed, heading out of Everdale. "Can't this thing go any faster?"

"It's a fuckin' goat! Of course it can!" Ryan jams into high gear and the heavier Buick soon begins to get smaller in the rearview. "Haha, yes!"

"I would not party so soon," Manuelo warns, pointing behind them to the Riviera hurtling up the road like a missile.

"Impossible," Ryan breathes.

The reaper-red Riviera bawls alongside them on their right and the driver points a shotgun out the window.

"*¡Estamos muertos!*" Manuelo cries.

The skeletal man fires the shotgun and blasts the Pontiac's rear window out.

"Shiiiiiiiit!"

Another blast blows half of the muscle car's rear end off, including a back tire, causing Ryan to lose control of the GTO and fly into a ditch. The car flips over and soars in the sky until it lands upside down in shambles.

Ryan looks around weakly, in the double-vision daze of a concussion, and listens to the engine rattle to a stop and begin hissing. He sees Manuelo bleeding from his forehead, eyes closed. Ryan tries to call Manuelo's name, but can't find the energy. Consciousness is quickly fading away. Before Ryan passes out, he sees a tall shadow coming down toward them, floating like a mystical seraph in black.

47

ONLY A FEW HOURS BEFORE DAWN, A LIGHT DRIZZLE falls on the Everdale City Cemetery, and a rumble, almost like thunder, builds in the misty air. The earthquake-like rumble is the sound of a death-red personal luxury vehicle at the locked iron gates, asking for admittance. It presses against the padlocked fence until the chain pops, and with a roar of success, the muscular Buick Riviera makes its way onto the cemetery grounds.

The vehicle rolls elegantly along, soon coming upon an empty grave that is coned and marked with crime scene tape. The driver of the brutal car is a tall man, his skin tightly stretched over his gaunt emotionless face and hairless scalp, giving him the appearance of a skeleton.

His left ear is almost completely missing, as if torn or bitten off, and his eyes are hidden behind dark shades. He is clothed from head to foot in black, save for grey lettering on his jacket that reads 'Live Good' above a creepy skull and 'Die Great' below. With no wasted movement or concern for the cool sprinkle that dampens his cheeks, the skeletal man gets out of the car and opens the trunk.

He crooks a thin finger for a bloody Ryan and Manuelo to climb out. They do so, trembling in the cold soft rain, their wounds from the accident aching and sore, waiting expectantly for the man to deliver their sentence. He remains mysteriously silent behind the dark sunglasses as he pulls a shovel from the Buick's trunk and offers it to Ryan.

Ryan recognizes the round pointed tool held in the blue-green hand as the same he had left in his now destroyed Chrysler. He eyes the skeletal man warily. Unwavering and unreadable, the man holds the shovel out in his bony right hand until Ryan tentatively reaches for it and accepts it.

"*Maldita mierda*, man," Manuelo moans. "Are you going to make us dig our own graves? Then bury us alive?"

This strikes Ryan as a very real possibility. "Aw, fuck *that!*" He drops the shovel on the ground like it was a writhing poisonous serpent.

"Pick that up!" orders the grim man. Ryan quickly stoops to collect the shovel and attempts to dry his brow with the back of his hand. The man walks around to the passenger side of his beastly car and carefully takes the corpse of Jeffrey Neil out, cradling the frail-looking body in his arms. "Get down there." The man nods to the open grave. Ryan looks around for a way out, but the man in black allows none. "Now!"

Ryan hops in the muddy hole, trying not to step on the broken casket that still lies inside. He shields his eyes from the steady downpour to look up for more instructions.

"Help me here," the man says to Manuelo. Manuelo assists with handing the corpse down to Ryan.

With great ceremonious care, Ryan lays Jeffrey back into the casket.

* * *

The rain has stopped, but Ryan and Manuelo's mud-covered clothes are still uncomfortably soaking in the first cool rays of the breezy daybreak. Ryan tosses the remaining sod on the now filled grave. The skeletal man sits perched on his dark car, gloomily watching as the job is finished. He grabs something from within a brown bag, and gets off the vehicle.

Ryan and Manuelo watch the man cautiously as he kneels down and props what Ryan recognizes as a Firebird emblem from an old Trans Am against the headstone. The man stays there on his knees in silence for a moment.

"He was a friend," the man says levelly from behind his concealing sunglasses. "He was a true friend." The man takes a slow ragged breath before proceeding. "He would put his life on the line for you, and he did for me. He earned his respect, when he was alive. It's no different now."

The man gets up and turns to the two teens. Ryan notices the gaunt man's face is contorted with grief, or maybe anger.

"When I saw what happened to his grave, what complete disrespect, I felt in a way, *I* was disrespected." He continues in a stronger voice hardened with ice. "I was going to kill whoever did this, whoever was involved. I was going to kill them and their families."

"Seems a little overboard," Ryan says.

"Well, when I was sitting over there, and the sun was coming up, and the birds were coming out, and my dead friend was being put in the ground…again…I still was going to do that."

"But you are okay now, right?" Manuelo asks.

The man gives a little shrug and shows his teeth in a smile. A smile like a weary jackal. "Killing you guys would be like strangling a couple puppies. I don't think that's what Jeff would have wanted." He shakes his head. "Besides, now I'm tired. And I have more important things to do."

A soft remembrance of half-formed images brushes across Ryan's mind, carrying with it a creeping suspicion. "...Adler?"

The skeletal man, his face returned to stone, walks over to Ryan and with his fiery red-orange hand, snatches the shovel away. He stares at Ryan from behind his shades and wipes the shovel off onto Ryan's shirt, then tosses it in the trunk. He climbs inside his car and fires it up, but rolls down the window to give Ryan and Manuelo a final word.

"Now this is the part where I'm supposed to give you some good advice." The skeletal man hits the gas to his gothic machine, it roars vociferously as its wide back tires kick mud all over the two teens, and it bellows out of the cemetery like a banshee, vanishing into the red and blue dawn.

Ryan stares after the car until the last sounds of its engine disappear, and the calm natural silence of the final resting grounds returns.

Manuelo is dumping mud out of his shoe. "What do you want to do?"

"I don't know yet," Ryan answers slowly, deep in reflection and looking at Jeffrey's grave under the wavering beams of morning that reflect off a nearby fountain, "but...I guess I'm free for anything." Nodding in agreement with his own thoughts, Ryan pulls a soggy mass of papers out of his pocket: Jeffrey's online journal.

He takes a knee by Jeffrey's headstone, and reads the inscription once again.

HE LIVED WITH THE HEART OF AN EAGLE

Ryan places the muddied journal pages under the emblem the warrior left behind. A light gust ruffles his damp clothes, and Ryan suppresses a shiver in the biting cold. "I'll miss you, Jeffrey," he says.

Dwelling on the quiet of the morning, Ryan absorbs the crushing weariness that weighs over his entire mind and body. He wipes his nose and stands up. Manuelo has his shoe back on and is waiting a few yards away next to a large statue. "Sorry about your car, Manuelo," he says.

"No big thing," Manuelo responds. "I have a Jaguar in Mexico."

"Oooh, that sounds gay." Ryan smiles, and the two friends start their trek out of the graveyard. "When are you going back?"

"Couple months. You got to come down to *D.F, cabròn*. The womans will treat you like a king. We will drink tequila all day, go to the clubs all night!"

"Well, like I said, I don't have anything keeping me here. I'm free to do anything," Ryan says, walking through the gates of the cemetery and out into the living world.

FANCY JACK CLANCY SAT IN HIS CAB ATTEMPTING to memorize the visuals within the pages of CREASE, while outside, the wind rustled through the trees and whistled between buildings. A storm was brewing in the night. The model in the glossy images suddenly made Fancy feel despondent. Her smile was phony and out of place.

He turned his melancholy gaze out the window, watching a dust devil stir up debris like his memories were stirring in his brain. He briefly thought on his past, mostly regrets, when he saw Wanda struggling against a burst of wind to push open the door of Fan Club UnLTD.

"Where does that nickel slot think she's going?" Fancy said, tossing the magazine onto the floor and stepping out of his car. "Wanda!"

Walking into the growing tempest, she stumbled and spun around to recognize Fancy as her caller.

"Where's my cheese, you scallywag *gape*?" Fancy yelled, rubbing his thumb and finger together, signifying money.

But Wanda didn't stay to chat, as she was already power walking in the opposite direction, with a hand blocking the massive amount of dirt blowing in her face.

Immediately giving chase, Fancy ran down the sidewalk after her. "I'm not a *john!*" he hollered as Wanda slipped around a corner. "*Or* your brother Juan!"

Fancy Jack snapped open his stiletto as he rounded the edge. "Wanda!" he tried to yell, but choked on a gust of filth that blew hard into his face. With squinted eyes, he went step by step against the current, pressing on a few yards before realizing he had lost sight of her. "You can't trick a treat, *see* sucker?" He squeezed the butterscotch horn of the knife, searching the shadows for his prey and shielding his eyes from the gale.

"This is unimaginable!" he chewed. "Unsubstantial! Un–" A grip like a bear trap clenched the back of Fancy's neck, chopping his words short. Numb and powerless, he was yanked into the passenger seat of an old car faster than he could utter a sound. The door of the vehicle slamming him in as it thundered down the road loud enough for the ground to split.

"Buckle up!" commanded a voice hard as iron.

When Fancy saw his kidnapper in the driver's seat, his blood turned to frost. In blind instinct, he lunged at the driver with his switchblade, shouting and stabbing at the throat.

"Mother fuckeeer!" the driver roared after blocking the thrust.

Fancy gawked in horror at the monstrous glee on the gaunt man's face, where there should have been indescribable pain. The blade had lodged hilt-deep in the man's green and blue tattooed forearm.

Fancy screamed and the driver in black screamed with him happily, pressing the gas closer to the floorboard, instigating the massive engine to pound down the highway.

"Not time yet!"

"I gave you plenty of *time*, Jack!" the driver spat, pulling a large handgun from underneath his seat. "Undeserved time."

"I didn't *do* anything!" Fancy shrieked as they sped through traffic so fast the other cars on the road began to blur.

The driver put the barrel to Fancy's head. "You never did."

Fancy moaned and his mind buzzed for an escape. He winced when the big car crashed through a barricade like a jackhammer on slush, caking the vehicle in a pale dust.

"There's nothing this way, cretin!" Fancy cried as they started to quickly ascend the unfinished 289 onramp that ceased abruptly in the sky. He ripped at the steering wheel, but the driver knocked him hard in the jaw.

"We're at the end of the road!" the driver growled. Folded in both hands like in prayer–he placed the gun to his own chin.

Blasting through the final blockades, Fancy went to buckle his seat belt, but found it missing with only gnawed ends.

At the height of paroxysm, fierce and calamitous, they rocketed toward the brink of the end.

RECOGNITION

THE AUTHORS EXTEND THANKS TO THE FOLLOWING
people for their part in the creation of this book:

Lloyd Garner, Jr., Lloyd Garner, Sr., Diane Sutton, Elizabeth Sassi
& Family, Winifred Stephens, Dave Stephens, Lindley Garner, Pam
Garner, Jason Downey, Dixie Hawks. James Newton, Jeong Lee,
Happy John Safin, Jeanne Lyet Gassman, Walter Goralski, Terry
Burns, Penina Keen Spinka, Jacques L. Condor, Jim Adams, Lisa
Lawrence, Michael Emery, and Dan Bentel & Family.

 ABOUT THE AUTHORS

DAX GARNER AND LLOYD GARNER ARE BROTHERS. They both earned a Bachelor of Arts from the Walter Cronkite School of Journalism and Mass Communication.